THE
Liminal
Space

THE
Liminal Space

JACQUIE MCRAE

First published in 2020 by Huia Publishers
39 Pipitea Street, PO Box 12280
Wellington, Aotearoa New Zealand
www.huia.co.nz

ISBN 978-1-77550-618-8

Copyright © Jacquie McRae 2020

Cover illustration copyright © Catherine Marion 2020

This book is copyright. Apart from fair dealing for the purpose of private study, research, criticism or review, as permitted under the Copyright Act, no part may be reproduced by any process without the prior permission of the publisher.

A catalogue record for this book is available from the National Library of New Zealand.

Published with the assistance of

For Sam, Dylan and Mitchell
Thank you for enriching my life

The liminal space:

The transitional space between

one point and the next.

The place where possibilities live.

William

WILLIAM

I walk to the library most days. The quiet there is different from the quiet at home; it's softer somehow, and not nearly as provoking. I don't need the books from the library, as sixty years of collecting have them scattered like birdseed around my house. My mother used to say that books were my hiding place, but for me, they are portals into other worlds. Stories have helped me understand who I am. Many have given me hope and shown me kindness when people around me have not. Books line my walls and spill from tables into small clusters onto the floor. When the books overflowed to the garden shed, I employed a local builder to construct some shelves. He presumed I was opening a second-hand bookshop and spread the word around the village. Soon after he finished, I would find people wandering among my shrubbery or popping out from behind a mulberry tree in their search for the shop.

The villagers excel at embellishing stories, and the fact that no one ever found the shop didn't deter them from adding to the story. They can dress a tale up so fine that it's hard to see the plain. The story of my arrival in the village of Radley is a classic example. Twenty years on and I still hear snippets about it in the market square. The most popular story has me turning up barefoot in the village, wearing ragged clothes and owning not much more than a mangy dog and several boxes of books. Rumour has it that I used to be a doctor with a practice in London, and I moved to the country when my wife died. I don't feel the need to tell them that I've never had a wife or a practice in London, and the closest they got to the truth was that, a lifetime ago, I did indeed use to be a doctor.

A warm clove-like smell from a vase of lilies greets me as I push open the library doors. The church owns the manse where the library is housed. The flowers from the service on Sunday get pride of place in the library on Monday. The vases are huge, and by the middle of the week, when the flowers are past their best, there's often a salty ham smell in the air, but it's still one of the nicest places to be in the village.

Emily steps out from behind a bookshelf in the romance section. To me, she appears white-petalled and yellow-centred, like the wild daisies that grow in the woodlands.

'Hi, William. Colleen put some books under the counter for you. I'll grab them.'

She reaches her thin little arms under the desk and taps around beneath it, like a house sparrow looking for crumbs. She struggles to lift the pile of books. I take them from her and shuffle through them as I wander over to the couch in the alcove. The couch is lumpy and uncomfortable, but at this time of day, the setting sun pours its warmth and light through the arched window directly onto it. It also acts like a crow's-nest, and I watch as Emily flits between the shelves.

From my vantage point, I see them all. From the broken people to the ones just looking for a way forward. I eavesdrop on their conversations and watch their eyes and the corners of their mouths for signs of how they're feeling. I want to yell out to them, tell them that they're not alone and that we're all afraid of something. I don't. I keep my head bowed and pretend to be reading the book resting on my lap.

EMILY

I leave work at the library early so I can buy chops, grill them and still have time for them to rest before serving. Rob likes to have his dinner on a tray in front of the six o'clock news. Maggie waves out to me as I rush along the cobblestone streets. You can hardly take a step in this village without bumping into someone who knows you. The lanes are one-way and circle back on themselves, so it's pointless even trying to hide. Maggie's been married to Reg, the postmaster, for over fifty years, and her claim to fame is winning the pancake race on Shrove Tuesday. I flick my hand in a wave but keep my head down and walk faster. I haven't got a spare hour to hear about Reg's gall bladder.

Most of the cottages in Radley cluster together, and our front doors open straight onto the pavement. The population grew so fast in medieval times that the builders ran out of dry timber for the new houses and used green beams. They warped when they dried, and now half the houses lean on each other for support. Just like the nursery rhyme, we all live together in our crooked little houses.

For thirty years, I've watched the goings-on in the village from my street-side bedroom window. I saw Mrs Beadle throw Mr Beadle's clothes out into the street, the night before he went overseas on a new job and then never came back. I witnessed Father John urinate on Mrs Buckley's prize roses and then weave his way back up to the church.

I grew up in this cottage with my grandmother. She left it to me when she died, but only because there was no one else to give it to. It wasn't until I married Rob nearly two years ago and he insisted we move into the master bedroom that I'd ever been inside her room. Until that day, her room and all of upstairs was out of bounds. I still feel like I'm breaking the rules, and some nights I feel like she's gazing down on me from the timber rafters. It makes me tense up and then everything turns weird between Rob and me. Rob's so practical. I can't imagine explaining to him about the ghost of a disapproving grandmother.

Winter is trying to come early. It's only October, and already I have to light the fire in the lounge to warm the place up before Rob gets in. I've barely got the onions and garlic diced when I hear him open the front door. He drops his keys and jacket onto the hall table. I listen to the sound of his footsteps as he walks across the floorboards, past the kitchen and into the lounge.

I wipe my hands on the front of my apron and then hang it on its hook. I measure seventy-five mils of whisky into a crystal tumbler and add three cubes of ice. I crouch and check my hair in the reflection on the oven door before taking him his drink. I place it on a coaster on the table beside him.

He doesn't look up but reaches out his hand for the glass before stabbing at a button on the remote.

'Dinner won't be long. We're having lamb chops.'

'Did you get the sauce?'

I close my eyes at my own stupidity. 'God, I forgot.'

Rob shakes his head.

'Do I need to write you a note or something? It's not that hard, is it? Lamb—Colman's mint sauce.' He sighs and drains the whisky.

I take his empty glass back to the kitchen. I can't believe that I've forgotten the sauce. It's like Rob said: Lamb—mint. Beef—dumplings. Chicken—gravy.

It's not that hard.

MARCO

I dress in a white pleated shirt and a black Armani suit and tie. I check my reflection in the mirror and note that my corkscrew curls could do with another cut. An inheritance from my Cuban side that I could do without. I slap on some Versace and inhale the woody scent before fastening my lucky cufflinks into the buttonholes. They need replacing: the luck seems to have dried up. I haven't sold a property in over a month.

I choose a posh restaurant in the heart of London to meet my clients for lunch. I want to sell them an apartment on Montague Square. From this rooftop restaurant, which has views along the Thames, I'll be able to point out their new abode. Punters love that. It's hard to find properties in this area, and I'm hoping that the small fortune I'll have to part with for lunch will come back in my commission cheque.

The minute I see his fake Jimmy Choo brogues step out of the black cab and get a look at the young tart he's brought with him, I know my time and money are about to be wasted. I cut the lunch short and drag them through the apartment. I know the drill. He pretends to be interested in buying and makes random comments about architectural features. She's stupid enough to be impressed. They go home and fuck, and I get fucked over.

I walk slowly back to our office, past the Regency-style buildings to Mountford Street. The floor-to-ceiling glass front makes our office look like an aquarium. It's not lost on me that inside the space, we act like Siamese fighting fish. Derek is already at his desk, his smirk firmly in place, ready for the fight.

'How'd you go, Marco? Get your sale?'

He says 'Marco' like he's getting rid of a bad taste in his mouth. He's always making racist slurs, and if he can get a shot in about Cubans, he will. His grin makes me ninety-nine percent certain that this morning was all a set-up. The one percent of doubt keeps my hands in my pockets, my mouth shut and my legs moving past his cubicle. I spend the afternoon at my desk willing my mobile to ring, and when it doesn't, I send out emails and look over my colleagues' advertising campaigns. At five I head for a bar on Oxford Street.

After a few bourbons, I notice the girl at the end of the bar. I take in her perky breasts, her manicured nails and the fact that she's downing drinks at the same rate I am. The bourbons have warmed me, and suddenly the day doesn't feel so bad. I move along the bar.

'Anyone sitting here?'

'No. Be my guest.' She removes her coat from the stool.

'I'm Nigel. Nice to meet you.'

'Funny, you don't look like a Nigel.' She raises her eyebrows at me and extends her hand. 'Marilyn.'

I shake her hand. 'You don't look like a Marilyn.'

We both smile. I notice the gaps in her front teeth, and see her looking at my Rolex. I spent my first commission cheque on the watch. It cost me more than my dad earns in his village shop in a month. It's been lean pickings lately, and I'm starting to regret some of my purchases. I thought I'd cracked it and the money would keep flowing. I'm a living cliché, spending my money on champagne, beautiful women and clothes.

I buy myself and Marilyn one more drink and then she follows me into the men's toilet. I call it a night straight after and walk back through the city streets to my apartment. Music blares from an upstairs bar. I weave my way past the people, who are milling around the doorway, hoping to get in.

I climb up the fire escape at the back of my building. I'm not in the mood to see my landlord. My rent's only a few weeks late, but the impatient cock harasses me daily about it. I'm sure he's laid a sensor wire under the carpet; it's been impossible to sneak past his door without him poking his ugly head out. I've been selling off my furniture to pay my rent, but I'm fast running out of things to sell.

I take the last container of noodles from the shelf and pour some boiling water over them. I prop myself up in bed while I eat and try to think of a cunning plan. If I don't come up with one, I'll have no choice but to head back to Radley. It's the place where I spent my childhood, dreaming about the day I'd get to leave. If I timed the traffic right, I could race there in the morning, coerce Dad into lending me some money and be back in the city by lunch.

JAMES

Mum and I stand together on the cobbled driveway and watch as Dad reverses his Jaguar out of the garage. He insists on driving us to the train station, although it's only a five-minute walk through the village and a minute across the overbridge.

'Don't be silly, James,' he said when I suggested we walk. 'How common would it look if we all traipsed through town dragging bags like a bunch of gypsies?'

He flicks open the boot, and I throw my suitcase in.

'Ready for the start of your life,' he says, looking at me in the rear-view mirror.

He takes it as given that my previous eighteen years count for nothing. I spread my lips into something I hope looks like a smile but say nothing. My acceptance letter into Oxford was the sign my father had been looking for that I wasn't a complete waste of space. He made a big production of going to the cellar and coming up with his oldest bottle of port to celebrate.

'To another lawyer in the family, and the fourth generation of Farndales to attend Oxford,' he said, raising his glass and toasting the air.

Mum's been doing her best to convince me that good times and lifelong friendships are on offer for everyone who attends, but I doubt that's true for me. My instincts have been telling me not to go—but remembering the look on Dad's face when I signed the letter acts like a clause on a contract and overrides everything else that's going on in my mind.

As the train is about to leave the station, something inside me screams to get off. Through the carriage window, I see my mother in her mustard housecoat and sensible shoes, standing as close as possible to the window and waving at me.

'I love you,' she mouths, and smiles for the first time in years, it seems.

It's the only thing that keeps me in my seat as the train pulls out.

EMILY

I glance at my watch as I race up the high street to work. To avoid the mortuary, I go the long way around. It's over a hundred years since the last body was wheeled into the rock cavern beneath the guildhall. Locked behind steel bars, the spiked metal trolley sits empty, but you know that the ghosts aren't too far away. My grandmother threatened to lock me in there for a night once, after I embarrassed her in public. She dragged me as far as the door, but I was saved by Mr Noonan walking his dog. I still wave out to him enthusiastically each time I see him; he's got no idea that he saved my life.

As I head up the hill, I think about last night and how I could have done things differently. I took my eyes off the chops for a second and they burnt. I had to scrape the black bits off, but they'd already tainted the meat. Rob took one bite before spitting it out.

'Jesus, Emily. Didn't anyone teach you how to cook?'

He knows damn well that there was nobody to teach me anything. I picked the meat up off the floor and took his plate out to the kitchen. The front door slammed a few minutes later, and I knew he'd be heading for the pub. I've never heard of anyone dying from breathing in whisky fumes, but some nights, as they puff from the side of his mouth, I wonder if I'll be the first.

I arrive at the library just as Colleen's unlocking the doors. She's been my boss for twelve years and appointed herself my stand-in mother long before that. She has an opinion about everything, especially if it involves me. She refused to come to my wedding because she didn't like the fact that Rob was way older and that we'd only been dating a few weeks before he asked me to marry him. I reminded her that she was the one who insisted I have a drink at the Swan after my grandmother's funeral. If it wasn't for her, I never would have met him. He said later that he'd been waiting there for over thirty years for me to turn up.

Colleen likes to say that she's worked at the library longer than Methuselah was alive. She's prone to exaggerating, but she's been here as long as I can remember. I was sent here as a kid to collect my grandmother's murder mysteries and to give her a break from me. While Colleen hunted along the shelves for my grandmother's books, I'd settle myself in the children's section. Each week Colleen handed me a book. It became our thing; I had to read ten books from each section before I got to move on to the next. I got stuck in the 900s, and Colleen jokes that history and geography are my specialist subjects, which isn't really funny, as I haven't even caught a train to London. Book by book, I read my way around the library, which is just as well, as it's the only education I got. I was home schooled on account of my easily corruptible genes. I knew about my crazy runaway mother, but I worried as a child that if we ever found out about the other half of my genes, I might not get to leave the house.

Every time I push open the oak doors and step into the library, something magical happens. I imagine it must be how Lucy felt when she walked through the wardrobe into Narnia. The world you were a part of a second ago disappears and is replaced by a wonderland of books. The library used to be the manse and has housed several ministers and their families, including the one who ran away with the offerings and someone else's wife. A houseful of furniture, wicker baby baskets, wooden rocking chairs, all got left behind. Some of the children etched their names into woodwork around the house, and I'm often putting books away and coming across a gouged-out Ezra or Bethany. I trace their names with my finger and make up stories about us being friends and sharing picnics by the river, where we chat about everything.

Each room houses a different part of our collection, and the groups that gather here all have their favourite spot. The ladies who are embroidering the new kneelers for the church like to sit around the AGA in the old kitchen. They often all talk at once and sound like the crows in the garden. The cookbooks sit on shelves that would have once held bottled peaches and pickled onions. The conservation group meets in the upstairs lounge surrounded by bookcases filled with books about nature and science. It has views out over the garden, and you can see the maples that line the path leading to the river. There was a big hullabaloo when the Royal British Legion club tried to pull rank and take over the lounge. Colleen prevented a battle by converting a bedroom into something that resembled a gentlemen's club. She chose the master bedroom, which had an ornately carved fire surround. She dyed the curtains black and reupholstered two wing-back chairs in a heavy brocade. Memorabilia was displayed in shadow boxes around the walls, and an old wooden drinks trolley was stacked with books about the various wars.

The iron beds in the children's rooms date back to the 1700s; they were forged by the local blacksmith and one of the ministers. The beds are made up with quilts and crocheted pillows donated by the Knit and Natter group. Several times we've found young children curled up and asleep in the folds of a blanket.

As soon as our doors open, Mrs Finlay bustles in. You could set the town clock to her movements.

'Morning, you two.'

'Hi, Mrs Finlay,' Colleen calls out from the kitchen.

'How are you this morning?' I ask, taking her carrier bag of books from her.

'Good, thank you.' She leans in close as I start returning her books. 'I've just heard that someone's coming to make a documentary about our little village. Isn't that exciting? I heard they chose us over those other people up the road.' She nods her head towards Bellingford, as if saying the name would break some sort of allegiance. She looks at me and smiles, but then frowns a second later. 'God, you look dreadful, Emily.'

'I don't know what to say to that, Mrs Finlay.'

'Sorry, but you do. Even your lovely brown curls are drooping. What have you been doing?'

'I think the honeymoon phase is over,' Colleen says as she places a cup of tea on the desk beside me.

'Surely not. It's only been a year—or is it two? Anyway, you probably just need more sex,' Mrs Finlay says, making Colleen snort and me blush.

Even the word makes me recoil.

It—sex—is nothing like I imagined it would be from the novels I'd read. It's closer to stories about a wild animal attacking its prey than any romance novel. The only difference is, in my case, when the beast has finished, he doesn't run off into the woods but flakes out beside me. Other than the fact that my body parts are involved, the whole thing could take place without me. I've opened my mouth a few times to say what I'm feeling, but Rob's not a guy you explain things to, and my words dry up somewhere before I can get them out anyway.

I make an attempt to smile back at the two of them. A huge part of me wants to ask them what I should do, but I know I should be able to figure it out on my own.

WILLIAM

I cradle the image of today's patient in my mind. Cup her gently in my thoughts as I meander up the path from my garden shed. I call them 'patients', but that's just habit; drop-ins or book borrowers describe them better. I don't encourage people to come, but they somehow find me. They arrive nursing wounds that have often been festering below the surface for years. I will them to look up and see the quote from Rumi that I painted above the door: 'The wound is where the light enters you.'

Often, their colours are jagged like someone has hacked at them with pinking shears. I've always seen people, and letters, in colours. My earliest memories are of my mother, who was sea-foam green, and my father, the deep reds of dried blood. I inherited the trait from my mother, as well as a few more. She explained it away as a mere blending of some senses. To her it was as mundane as the fact that my hooked nose came from Grandma Lake. But it's always made me feel flawed, as if there was something inherently wrong with me.

Juno, my chocolate Lab, appears from the side of my house and bounds towards me. Her tail whips at the wild flowers growing beside the path. She slobbers on my sleeve, and her tongue licks my hand. She's got no sense of time; her welcome is the same whether I've been gone five minutes or five hours. I scratch between her ears and see the gratitude in her tail.

'Hey, Juno.'

She trails me up the path, making sure I don't deviate from finding her food. I stoop down and gather an armload of wood from the side of the house. I push the front door open with my foot, and Juno sneaks in before the wind slams it shut behind us. Balthazar meows and smooches past me on the way to his front-row seat by the fire. I lean forward and let the pile of logs fall from my arms into the copper tub.

The smell of chicken wafts from the kitchen. I'm not hungry, but I ladle a cup of soup from the Crock-Pot into a bowl. I slump down in my armchair and rest the bowl in my lap. I blow lightly on the soup, more out of habit than a need to cool it.

The light from the table lamp casts an amber glow around the room. On the first day that I moved into the cottage, I climbed up a ladder and took all the overhead light bulbs out. I couldn't stand the harshness of the light and couldn't think of any reason to have everything illuminated at once.

I watch the flames of the fire leap around, imitating my thoughts. I return to the image of today's patient in my mind and move to the bookshelf. My fingertips shuffle across the spines of the books. One of them holds a message, but I'm not sure which one. Usually, I can prescribe a book for someone on a first meeting; a thought of what I could give them is forming as they're talking. Today I had a block, and tonight a sharp pain in the middle of my temple means that I'm having trouble following a thought through to the end.

I doze in my armchair until the cold wakes me in the early hours. I brew a pot of tea and take it to my writing desk. I roll up the mahogany top and finger some sheets of coloured paper before settling on the yellow. I slide a sheet into an old typewriter that belonged to my mother. I love the feeling of the cold curved typewriter keys beneath my fingertips. The tap, tap sound as my thoughts are transferred to paper. A purging: freeing up space for the new thoughts. My mother taught me to jot down my thoughts as soon as I could write. It was her way of channelling my tendency to blurt out whatever came to me into something more acceptable. My thoughts—there was something ugly inside Uncle Bill, or Mavis next door was going to die soon—were rerouted onto pages and never spoken out loud. My father too encouraged me to 'keep my mouth shut'. I sometimes thought I'd suffocate on all the words I never got to say.

I type until I see the upper edge of the sun appear on the horizon.

I take my coat from the stand by the front door and tuck the book I've chosen into a pocket. I'm ambushed on the porch by Juno, a muddy boot clenched in her mouth. She drops it at my feet and runs off to find her lead. The light is still dim, and streamers of mist are strung between the rooftops. There's a certain kind of quiet that rests in the village at this hour of the morning. Like a set on a stage before the actors walk on and take over.

I notice a ball of colour in the distance, and as I get closer, I recognise the forest green of my neighbour Arlo. We share an apple tree at the bottom of our gardens. It's old and doesn't bear much fruit, but it provides the perfect amount of shade. Beneath its gnarly branches, afternoons have disappeared as we've traded stories and tried to make some sense of the world. Having Arlo to talk to, knowing that he doesn't judge me, has been one of the best gifts I've ever been given.

I call out to him now, and he pauses at the crossroads for me to catch up. I nod towards the box of veggies that he's carrying. 'Where are you off to so early?'

'It's Wicked Wednesday.' He winks before heading off up the street.

I head down towards Water Street. In the guildhall, there's a photo of the street when one of the tributary rivers used to flow straight down it. Mrs Finlay said it was her great-grandfather who came up with the idea of diverting the water under the road, through a pipe and into the wool factory that made the town famous. I stop at one of the houses built on top of the culvert and slide the book through the mail slot. Along the street, Agnes is struggling to drag her husband inside the house. A broken bottle and an impression of a body shape are obvious in her flower bed. Across the hedgerow that separates their backyards, Rowena yells out to her neighbour.

'Just leave him where the good Lord flung him, Agnes.'

I quicken my step. Two veteran oaks act as sentries at the entrance to the woodlands. I bow my head in a greeting to both. At the kissing gates, I unleash Juno, and she licks at my hand before racing off into the woods. Branches of alders arch over the path and reach like lovers to entangle with the branches on the other side. Rays of morning light filter down through the canopy, and the scent of sweet honeysuckle fills the air. As I wander through the cathedral of trees, I let out a long sigh.

My shoulders release down and my face relaxes. I take my shoes off and feel the leaves and the earth beneath my soles. I scrunch up my toes a few times and then stand still and soak up the woodlands. They seep in through all my senses, and a calmness settles over me. I'm aware of the in and out of my breath. With my eyes closed, I inhale the smell of pine and feel the coolness on the inside of my nostrils. I can hear a melancholy cry from a bullfinch in the distance. There's a rustle near my feet, and I open my eyes in time to see a dormouse scurrying away beneath some leaves. I wander along the path, pausing at the end of each step. I'm in no rush.

The fluffy spikes of goldenrod wave out to me from the edge of the woodlands. Most people consider it a weed, but I love the flash of sunlight colour and the plant's determination to strive in the poorest of conditions. I pick some flowers before getting distracted by the scarlet of nearby rosehips. I snip a few of those stems and admire the way they lace themselves so tightly into the hedgerows.

I stop at the library on my way back and place the flowers in a shaded part of the porch. I leave a scribbled note for Emily and Colleen before tucking it under the flowers so it can't blow away.

The main street is now swarming with cars and people. A group of tourists is taking selfies with cameras perched on long metal sticks outside the leaning Tudor-style shops. A car takes up two parks on the narrow cobblestone street. I recognise the man at the wheel as Arlo's son, Marco. His colours of burnt orange with slashes of midnight blue couldn't belong to anyone else. I wave out to him, but he's yelling into his mobile phone and doesn't notice me. I'm still looking at the car window as I step onto the road. It's in that moment that the delivery van pulls into the same space.

Then there is no colour.

MARCO

'Fuck, I've gotta go. Some fuckin' moron just stepped out in front of a van.' I put the phone on the seat and look around, hoping that someone else will go to his aid.

The van driver's out of his vehicle and yelling at the guy on the road but making no sense at all. As I go to the front of my car, I see that the moron has pushed himself up to sitting.

'Marco?'

'William?'

Shit. Blood is pouring from a gash on his head. First I get stuck in traffic, and now this. I'm careful not to get any blood on my suit as I lean down.

'Jesus, William. Are you alright?'

'Yes. I just lost my vision for a second.'

I place my hands under his arms to pull him up, but he's so light I nearly throw him skywards. He's lost heaps of weight since last time I was home.

The guy from the van jumps back in his vehicle and roars off.

'Fuckin' idiot,' I say to his tail lights. 'Come on, William, I'll drop you at the doctor's.'

'I'm okay. I can walk.'

'Yeah, Dad would like to hear that I let his best friend walk to the doctor's after a van hit him. Come on.'

I open the door to my car and push him in from behind. This little accident may well work in my favour. I drive for two minutes before stopping alongside the thatched cottage that houses the doctor.

A nurse rushes William into one of the cubicles when she sees the blood dripping from his head.

A girl behind the desk slaps some papers on the counter. 'Fill out this form,' she says before looking up at me.

'Marco?'

'Kay.'

Fuck. Kay Baxter. A girl I didn't date but slept with several times in high school. She reminds me why I don't come home much.

'I haven't seen you around for a while. Are you still selling real estate in London?' Her big smile is desperate, and I note that she's not wearing a wedding band. I could still be in if I wanted.

'Yeah. It's really busy. I'm just here for a day.'

'That's a shame. Maybe we could catch up next time.'

'Yeah, maybe.'

'I'm here Mondays and Tuesdays. Oh, and at the Swan on Friday and Saturday nights.'

I nod and take a seat as far away from the desk as possible. I don't plan on being around long enough to need her.

JAMES

Red ivy creeps along the parchment-coloured walls of the university building. The grotesques carved from stone glare at me from their posts along the top of the wall. A sense of unease weaves its way through my body and out into my clammy hands. My heart starts racing as I try to keep pace and concentrate on the information my appointed buddy is firing at me.

'Mix 'n' mingle at seven in the common room after dinner, which is served in the dining room at five,' he tells me, pointing to some buildings in the distance. 'Library that way, arts building that way,' and then he switches to quadrants and handbooks … blah, blah, blah. My thoughts are all over the place, and I don't trust myself to speak. I keep nodding like some car ornament, and I see him look at me strangely. I'm relieved when he unlocks the door to my room and instructs me to 'unpack and get ready for the evening'.

My suitcase topples onto the dark wooden floorboards, and I sink down onto the bed. My room's not much bigger than my wardrobe at home, and a feeling of claustrophobia descends on me. I open the small leadlight window to let some light in, but it only opens a fraction, caught by the trunk of a giant maple.

I check the time on my new mobile.

'We'll be able to keep in touch daily,' Mum assured me as she handed me their gift.

'I think that James will probably have better things to do than phone his mum each day.' Dad winked at me, which made Mum blush.

I hang up my clothes and unpack my things into the drawers. I move the lamp around the desk before settling it on the left-hand side and lay my pens alongside it. I'd thought of bringing a memento from home, but I couldn't think what it should be. I check my phone and see that only five minutes have passed since last time I looked. I flop onto the bed and stare at a black smudge on the ceiling. I think about the other people who must have stared at this same spot and wonder what they were thinking. Did they too question what the hell they were doing here?

A bell rings in the distance; I have no idea what it's for. God, I hope it's not a fire bell. I hear the sound of voices and people walking past my door. I poke my head out as two girls walk past. There is a huge noise coming from a room at the end of the hallway.

'Come on,' one of the girls calls over her shoulder to me. I force myself to follow them. People are everywhere. A spindly girl with cropped red hair stands on a chair and shouts at people to be quiet. The guy next to me makes a face and yells out to his mate across the room. I untuck my collared shirt when I see everyone else is in jeans and casual shirts. I have a special knack for never blending in. A gap opens up in the throng of students, and, without thinking, I move into it. It closes around me, and I'm trapped in a wall of people. I stand on my tiptoes and look for an exit but can't find a way out. There's a tightening in my chest, and I try to suck in more air. Tingling starts in my fingers, and I freeze as it travels up my arms. Something is really off. Numbness crawls up my neck and takes over my head. I feel like I'm thickening, and the room starts to spin. I want to sit down, but I know I'd suffocate if I did. I have to get out.

I don't understand what's happening. I try to say something, but I have no saliva, and my tongue feels swollen and isn't moving. I push people out of the way, and some of them shove me back. My heart thumps against the inside of my chest. I must be having a heart attack. God, is this dying? Shit, I need air. I stagger out to the quadrant and slump down onto the grass. My breathing is forced, and my in-breath is a gasp. My limbs feel heavy and immovable, but another part of me is restless and urges me to stand up and keep moving.

A girl walks over to me, but I wave her away and keep pacing. My fast movements fan cool air onto my face. Slowly, the world tilts back onto its axis. I notice the rain and a crowd of people watching me from the shelter of a stone archway. One of them yells out, but I can't hear what he's saying. I turn and walk in the opposite direction.

I find my way to the river and slide down the bank. I sit on the grassy verge and watch the steady flow of water. I used to believe, as a boy, that the river had magical powers. The colder the water, the stronger the power. For a moment, I think about walking down into the river, but then I feel my shoulders relax, and my breathing returns to normal. I cradle my head in my hands. What the hell just happened? I haven't been here for twenty-four hours, and already I've messed up. Marked myself as the weird guy.

I wait for the cover of darkness before winding my way along a path and back to my room. I pull off my wet clothes and leave them in a pile on the floor before climbing into bed. A chill has seeped into my body; I wrap my arms around myself to warm up.

A bell rings out in the morning, but I can't make myself get up. A few hours later, I feel pains in my stomach and remember that the last time I ate was on the train. I force myself to walk to the dining hall for lunch. I take a seat at one of the long tables. Tingling starts in my arms. *Please, God, not again.* My heart starts racing, and I can feel myself panicking as my breathing goes all funny. I run outside and head for my room.

A feeling of heaviness pins me to my bed in the morning, and I miss my first class. My stomach still doesn't feel right, and the thought of food makes me nauseous. I touch my forehead, looking for signs of a fever, but it feels normal. I make myself get dressed and take the main path from my dorm to the lecture hall. I pull the hood of my duffel coat over my forehead as far down as it will go.

'Hey, Rain Man,' someone calls out to me, which makes the others in the group laugh. I tilt my head further down and walk briskly to the hall. In class, I hear whispers and presume they're talking about me. I can feel my body starting to tense up, and I leave before the lecture finishes.

I tell myself that it must be nerves and it'll pass. I keep hoping that I'll feel better and able to cope, but each morning I wake up with the same sense of dread. I have to curl up to get away from it. The light and the dark come and play on the walls.

I ignore the knocks on my door. I hear muffled voices outside but can't make out what they're saying. At some point, there are people beside me. Someone shines a light in my eyes, and I hear someone calling for a doctor. I take the slide into oblivion.

My name gets to be written in the family history books, as the first Farndale to be asked to leave Oxford.

EMILY

I start the pie early and have it in the oven ready to be turned on. I can't believe it's my second wedding anniversary already. Earl cut me a prime piece of steak and found some lovely pigs' kidneys from out the back. Rose said the key to a good steak-and-kidney pie was to make sure the suet was well shredded. I shredded it, chopped it and then used the stick blender for good measure.

I put everything away and wipe the benches clean.

I didn't bother telling Colleen the truth. It was easier to say that I had a dentist appointment and needed to leave work early than to say that I wanted to get home and clean up. She doesn't understand about trying to keep husbands happy.

I set the alarm on the kitchen timer for ten minutes and slide into the bath. I lie back and disappear into the steam clouds. My skin instantly goes red, but I don't mind. After having to use my grandmother's cold bathwater for most of my life, a little red is a sign of victory. I wish she was alive to see that I did get a husband, in spite of all her predictions.

The pie is perfect, and my mood lifts a little as I put the plates in the oven to warm. I place a tea light in a small jar in the middle of the table and polish the knives and forks as I lay them down. I push the crystal tumbler a fraction closer to Rob's place setting. The clock chimes seven, and I start to worry that the pie might dry out. I wait five minutes and then take it out of the oven and wrap it in aluminium foil. I baste a little egg and milk over the top of the pie at eight, and then at nine cut a sliver for myself. The grandfather clock chimes ten as I blow out the candle. I fold a piece of paper in half and write 'Happy anniversary' then balance the note on top of the ruined pie.

A few hours later, I hear him as he crashes up the stairs. I ignore him when he calls my name and pretend to be sleeping when he comes into the room. I bite down on my bottom lip to stop myself crying. *Don't you dare cry,* I tell myself. *You'll make it worse.* I press down harder.

I wake early, and I'm at the library by seven, which was the time I used to get here when my grandmother was alive. Colleen bought me my own set of keys for my sixteenth birthday. She said it wasn't a good look to have me sitting on the stone steps every morning, waiting for her to arrive. I stayed overnight a few times, but we both pretended I didn't. I take the feather duster from the hall cupboard and knock down a few spiders setting up house along the beams. I move a chest of drawers in the children's room and take books off the shelves to use for a display.

'Morning,' Colleen calls out as she arrives. Five minutes later, she brings me a cup of tea.

'What have you done to your lip, Emily?'

My tongue automatically runs over the blood blister.

'I must have done it in my sleep.'

She frowns at me and sits down on one of the beds. As she sips her tea, she looks at me over the rim of the cup.

'What's the display?' She nods her head towards the books on the ground.

'I thought I'd do a medieval theme. Every second kid wants the *Frozen* books. I thought I'd highlight some other prince and princess stories.'

'You know it's not true, right?'

'What?'

'That a knight in shining armour comes and rescues you.'

I ignore her and spend the rest of the morning making props for my display. I fold cardboard into castles and model clay into moats. I use the metal soldiers and horses that we found in a biscuit tin under the stairs. I envy the child who was given these treasures. They must have cost a fortune; it would have taken someone hours to hand-paint all the details onto the soldiers' uniforms and the gold lettering onto the horses' capes. Colleen thinks that the toys are at least a hundred years old.

Ivy bustles in and heads straight for the kitchen to make herself a coffee. She seems to have got things a bit twisted since she became chairperson of the church committee. Colleen says you'd think she personally owned the library the way she carries on. I watch now as Colleen follows her into the kitchen, and I wait for the fireworks to start up. It takes just a few minutes.

Ivy comes storming out.

'I'm sorry, but we have no choice.'

'What nonsense, Ivy. We always have a choice.'

I have to sidestep Ivy to avoid a collision. She scowls at me as though I'm the one rushing around like a bull.

'You should get rid of those weeds too, Emily.' She nods towards the wild flowers that William so thoughtfully left on the porch. 'Some of them look poisonous.'

I'd love to tell her that she's the only poisonous thing I see, and that she could do with being a bit thoughtful herself.

WILLIAM

The nurse dabs at the blood trickling from my head wound. Relief floods through me as she ushers me into the cubicle. A waiting room is the worst place for someone like me. The space between myself and other people can get blurred. My body mirrors the sensation or pain in someone else. I feel their broken arm in mine, or the tightness of their breathing in my chest. I have to quickly shift my focus to stop feeling the sensations the other person is feeling. I've learnt some skills to protect myself, but if there are too many people at once, I can get overwhelmed. I felt a seismic shift as a child when I discovered that not everyone viewed the world in quite the same way as me. I was thrown to the edge of the world, and I've been waiting to fall off ever since.

'Take a seat, William. I'll check your blood pressure and clean out that wound before the doctor sees you.' She wraps a cuff around my upper arm and looks at the gauge, then looks back up at me. 'I don't think I've ever seen you in here?'

'No. You wouldn't have.'

'120 over 80. Perfectly normal.'

I'm wondering if there's such a thing as imperfectly normal when a doctor pulls the curtain back.

'Hi. I'm Doctor Barnaby. I'm filling in while Doctor Moore is on holiday. I hear you're a lucky man.'

I nod. It seems a funny thing to say to a man who's just been hit by a van. He flicks some surgical gloves on and peers at the gash.

'This looks fine. Just give it a couple of butterfly stitches,' he says to the nurse. He pulls an ophthalmoscope from his pocket and examines my eyes.

'Your son said you lost your vision for a moment?'

'He's my neighbour's son. I lost it for a second.'

'Mm-huh.' The doctor keeps the light shining into my eyes. 'I'm sure it's nothing to worry about, but I'd like to run a few more tests.'

'What is it you're worried about?'

'Well, the optic nerve looks a little swollen. Have you been having any headaches before this accident?'

'A couple.'

'Best we rule out a few things. I'll make a referral, and a nurse will be in touch with you. For the moment, just go home and rest.'

I gather my coat. I'm surprised to see Marco still sitting in the waiting room. He stands up as soon as he sees me and heads towards the door.

'Excuse me, William,' the girl behind the counter calls out to me. 'We need a few more details.'

'I'll come back later. I'm too tired now.' I turn towards Marco. 'Thanks for waiting. I appreciate it.'

Marco grabs my arm and shepherds me out. In a few minutes, we're parked in his dad's driveway.

'Thanks again, Marco. Tell your dad I'll talk to him later.' I get out and slip through the hole in the hedgerow. I cut a space out of it when Marco was little so he could come and go between our houses.

The smell of white sage and rosemary greets me as I open the front door. The familiar smells comfort me. I put another log on the fire while Balthazar and Juno supervise. I brew a pot of peppermint tea and take it into the lounge. The light streams in through one of the windows as I place the typewriter on a coffee table in the sunshine. I pick my words carefully; cradle them for a while before I set them down on paper. I stop typing when my thoughts become foggy and a pain between my shoulder blades means I need to stretch. Juno comes over and rests her head by my knee. I stroke the back of it.

'Don't worry, we'll be fine.'

MARCO

I see Dad through the glass door, sitting in an old tartan chair, a cup of tea on a side table and the newspaper folded in quarters across his lap. I have to bash on the door and yell for ages before he turns around and notices me.

'Jesus, Dad, get a friggin' doorbell or some hearing aids.'

'Nice to see you too, Marco. Your mother would die if she heard you talking like that.'

I shake my head. Dad talks about Mum as if she's just popped out for a moment, but she ditched us years ago. He's been trying to cover for her ever since. I think the silly bugger still hopes that she'll come back. I wouldn't cross the street to say hi.

In the kitchen, I flick the kettle on to make a coffee.

'Do you want one?'

'I've got one, thanks. How's the big city?'

'Same. Big.'

'And your job?'

I pretend not to hear and make a production of banging things around on the bench.

'I just brought William home from the doctor's,' I say as I take a seat beside him.

'Our William?'

'No. Someone else's William. Of course our William. He stepped in front of a van outside McCarthy's.'

'God. Is he alright?'

'Yeah, apparently he will be.'

'Ooh. What a thing to happen.' Dad shakes his head in disbelief. 'I better go see him.'

'He said to let you know that he's fine and that he's having a rest. I had to wait at the doctor's for over an hour.'

'That's nice of you, Mijo.'

The term of endearment is my cue.

'Dad, I need your help with something. I need to borrow some money.'

Dad sits back in his chair and looks directly at me.

'What for, Marco? Doesn't your fancy job pay you well?'

'The market's pretty slow, but I'm sure it'll pick up. I just need to borrow some money to get me through.'

'Don't you have any savings?'

'No, Dad, I don't; that's why I'm asking for the loan.'

I have to get up and move around, as his questions irritate me so. I take the cups back to the kitchen.

'How much do you need?'

'About 2000 pounds should do.'

'I could live off that for a year. What do you need that much for?'

'Rent's overdue on the apartment, lease on the car, gym membership. Jesus, Dad. Can you loan me the money or not?'

'It's not about the money, Marco. Maybe you need to look at some of the choices you make.'

I have to bite down on the side of my gums to stop myself from having a crack.

'I didn't come for a lecture. I've got to get back to the city. Can you do it or not?'

'I need to think on it.'

The screen door closes behind him as he goes out to his veggie plot. When Mum left, he dug up the entire back garden and put in vegetables. Kids at school teased me that my mum hadn't left but was buried at the back of our house. Whenever Dad needs to think, he gardens.

I look around at Dad's pathetic lot. The salmon-coloured couch that he picked up from the side of the road was one of his favourite finds. 'We now have something to sit on,' he said, beaming, as he dragged the ripped thing into our lounge. Every pathetic prize I've ever won is on display in a special cabinet that he got from a gala day. He paid a pound for it, and even though it was missing its glass front door and every panel on it was a different colour, it was the focal feature in our lounge.

Dad's penchant for picking up other people's throw-outs became a business. For the past fifteen years, he's had Arlo's at the bottom of the main street. You'd have thought he'd won the lottery when he signed the lease on the shop. He sells second-hand goods and veggies.

I slump down into Dad's chair and unleash a hit of Cuban cigar smell. I guess I'm not getting back to work today.

JAMES

Mum comes into my room and pulls the curtains back.

'Good morning, James,' she says in a fake cheery voice. 'Come and have some breakfast.'

I drag my clothes from the floor and struggle into them. Dad's seated at the table and halfway through his morning cup of coffee. He's the only lawyer in the village and clerk of the parish council. He's dressed, as always, in a dark suit, a white shirt and a dark tie.

He looks at me over the top of his newspaper. It's weeks since I came home, and I can still catch traces of a certain look on his face. The look he had when he came to collect me from school.

I do feel sorry for him. I was meant to be brilliant, or at least have some sporting abilities. His line ends at useless.

I move the crockery around the table and force myself to spoon in a couple of mouthfuls of cereal. As we pass butter, honey and pleasantries, I see my mother's eyes searching mine for signs that I may be getting well. I widen my mouth into something like a smile and hope that the gesture eases some of her suffering. I see her face relax a little.

'There's a meeting in the library tonight to discuss the church restoration,' Mum says as she flicks her napkin onto her lap. 'Apparently, the footings are all collapsing. It could cost thousands of pounds to fix them.'

'They should have thought about that before they wasted money on those ridiculous stained-glass windows.'

'Beth Stone donated most of the money for the windows.'

'Buying her way in will be the only way that woman will get to heaven. Anyway, I've still got no sympathy for the church. I told them that money would be better spent on a brass plaque with the names of our forebears, but they didn't listen to me.'

'What do you think, James?'

I sense Dad watching me across the table.

'Sorry. I wasn't really listening.'

'Mmm. I think, James, that it would be a good idea for you to start participating in a few things.' He nods his head in agreement with himself. 'Maybe start with some exercise.'

He stares at me, and I wonder if he's expecting some kind of enthusiastic response.

'Perhaps running. Obviously, you'll have to start with small distances, but it's something you could start today.'

'Maybe.'

'Did you have something else on, James?'

Most things seem to float above Mum, but even she flinches.

'No, but I don't feel that great today.'

'Well, I'm sorry about that, but I think getting moving may help.'

'Right.' I can't think of anything else to say.

'Maybe a walk to the river,' Mum says enthusiastically. 'You used to love the river.' I see her smile, so full of hope. I want to give something back to her.

'Yeah, maybe.'

'I could come with you this morning,' she says.

Dad throws Mum a look. I'm not certain what it means, but I know that he doesn't think it's a good idea.

'I'm fine, Mum. I can go on my own.'

WILLIAM

The bell above the post office door clangs loudly as I enter. Reg leans over the counter as he talks to his wife Maggie, and his voice drops to a whisper when he sees me. It's rare to see them apart, and their oranges and reds bubble together like molten lava rushing down a mountainside. Maggie used to have a little gift shop in one corner of the post office, but it's slowly taking over the shop. There seem to be more crocheted hats, cushion covers and stuffed animals every time I come.

Reg straightens himself up and fires mail into the wooden post boxes that line the wall. He avoids making eye contact with me and sets his mouth into a tight-lipped grimace. Maggie takes herself off to the other side of the shop and arranges a family of knitted mice on a shelf while still keeping an eye on me. I see the way she does the body scan, from my scuffed leather brogues all the way up to my unkempt beard and tangled hair that hasn't seen a comb in years. Her eyes tell me that she finds me lacking in some way. I flick through my mail and crumple up a blue flyer. Reg slips church propaganda into the mailboxes most days. I toss it in the waste-paper bin on my way out. They'll be talking about my express pass to Hell as soon as I leave the shop.

I step onto the pavement, and Juno immediately stands up and takes the lead. I smile as she bustles her way up the high street. She heads for the meadow behind the library. Up ahead I see Mrs Ester glance my way, and I'm happy when she crosses the street. Any contact with her feels like fingernails being dragged across a blackboard. I pause for a moment at the old railway bridge and look out across the tree-fringed meadow. The lichen-covered post with the sign marking the way has fallen over into the long grass. We walk for a few minutes beside the hedgerows until we come to an embankment. I climb over it, Juno following, and half walk, half slide down the other side. At the bottom, by the river, I take off my shoes and roll up the hem of my trousers. I leave my shoes on top of a rock and amble across the ancient ford. The cold water seeps into my trousers and bites sharply at my toes. I wrap my frayed coat tightly around me. From here you can see three of the tributary rivers flowing into the Athena. I fill my flask from a spring that trickles down a ravine and then settle beside a lone black poplar. Juno lies down beside me. I take my notebook and pencil from my pocket and scribble a few lines. I lean back on the grass and close my eyes. The soft rumble as the water tumbles over the rocks lulls me to sleep.

A Muscovy duck yanking on the edge of my coat, and voices from people on the river walkway, wake me up. As my eyes adjust to the light, I look across the river and see a shape under the bridge. At first I think it's a small boulder, but then I realise it's a crouching person. Their arms are wrapped around their knees. It looks like a young man, but it's hard to tell, as they're obscured by an old willow tree. The wind blowing the leaves distracts me as it rustles its mournful tale.

What starts as a dull thud in my temple intensifies, and I have to move. I remember a bush of feverfew I saw by the side of the bridge on my way down. A few of the leaves steeped in hot water should make my headache subside. I cross back over the river and clamber halfway up the bank. The person is still crouched here; it is a young man.

'Hello.'

He jumps up, and I see that I startled him.

'I'm sorry. I didn't mean to frighten you.'

Without saying anything, he steps behind a boulder. I shrug and climb further up the bank to the bush. As I pick a handful of leaves, I remember the boy's face and realise that he's the lawyer's son. Juno decides to use that moment to race back down and check out a possible new companion. I call her and am surprised when she doesn't return. I have to traipse all the way back down.

'Sorry,' I say, walking around the boulder and grabbing Juno by her collar. 'You probably don't remember me, but I used to meet you and your mum on the riverbanks when you were a boy. I'm William, and this is Juno. I'm afraid she doesn't see the point of manners. James, isn't it?'

He nods without really looking at me and walks away. I suffer an overwhelming sense of compression, like the air above me is pushing me down. Sadness rested in the corners of his mouth. He didn't let me see his eyes, and a part of me is grateful. Juno looks up at me and whines. 'I know you want to follow, but we're not invited.' We scramble up the bank and walk the path home. I feel like I'm dragging my legs, and it takes a few minutes for the heaviness in my body to subside and for me to let go of the boy's muddied colours. I'm momentarily confused when I open my garden gate and a female voice calls out to me from my back porch.

'I was just going to leave you a note, William.'

It's the girl who was behind the counter at the doctor's yesterday. She waves a piece of paper in the air as she walks towards me.

'We don't have a phone number or email for you, so I thought I'd just drop by. We got you an appointment in a few weeks, but I couldn't book you in because I didn't have your NHS number. I typed "William Newton" into the database three times, but I still couldn't find you.'

'It's probably just entered in the system wrong. I'll pay them cash on the day,' I say.

'Yes, that's fine, but they'll still need a number to process it.'

'It'll be somewhere inside. I can give it to them.'

'I'm on a break, so I'll just wait here till you find it.' She sits down on a log seat that Arlo made from a tree that came down in the last storm. She stares across the fence into Arlo's kitchen.

'I'm sorry. What was your name again?'

'It's Kay.'

'Right. Sorry, Kay. It could take me a while to find it. I'm not one for paperwork.'

'That's okay, William. I can come back tomorrow.'

'No. I'll bring it to you when I find it. It'll be buried under something in the office.'

She looks disappointed, but finally leaves. I let out a long breath that I didn't realise I was holding.

EMILY

I light the fire in the kitchen and throw the lamb mince into a bowl along with some rosemary and thyme. I heard Rob tell someone that he married me for my shepherd's pie. I throw the potatoes in a pot and turn the element on to hot. I jump when I hear the front door slam.

Rob surprises me by coming into the kitchen. He throws a brown package on the table.

'I got you this,' he says, nodding down at the parcel.

I wipe my hands on my apron and pick up the parcel like it's a newborn baby.

'I can't believe you brought me a present,' I say, grinning like I've won at the fair. 'Is it an anniversary present?'

'Can be. Open it then.'

I undo the string slowly and pull back the paper on one side. I spy something red. He remembered my favourite colour. I see it's shiny and then notice some black lace. I pull out a negligee and feel the grin slip from my face.

'What, don't you like it?'

'Yeah, no, thank you. I just thought it was something else.' I turn away from him so he can't see the disappointment on my face. I pull the potatoes off the stove. 'I better get these potatoes mashed, or you'll be eating late.'

'Is there a problem?'

'No, no, Rob. You go into the lounge. Dinner's nearly ready.'

I push the ugly thing back into the paper and put it on the sideboard. I can't believe I let myself think I'd be getting a real present. I take him his dinner and eat mine by the fire in the kitchen. After dinner, I wipe all the cans in the pantry and check all the spices for their expiration dates. When I hear the theme music for the dart show, I creep off to bed. I'm nearly asleep when I hear the floorboards creak on the stairs, and my whole body stiffens.

He flicks the light on, and I feel something land on the bed.

'Go try it on then.'

I pretend to be asleep, but he pulls the covers back and shoves my shoulder.

'Go on.'

It's easier not to argue. I force myself into the bathroom and pull the negligee over my head. I catch a glimpse of myself in the mirror; I feel so ugly. I pull the material up to cover my breasts, but then it exposes my lower half. I tug at the hem as I walk back into the bedroom.

'You'll bloody rip it if you keep doing that.'

I let the hem drop, and I walk towards the light switch.

'Hang on. Let me look at you.'

I turn around and keep my hands down beside me. I feel the heat in my face and will myself to feel something other than stupid.

'Actually, your boobs are too small for the top, and your ribs are sticking out. Turn the light out.'

MARCO

I'm usually the last to arrive at the office, but this morning I'm seated at my desk long before Owen gets in. I'm hoping that he didn't notice my absence yesterday. He looks directly at me as he walks into the office and beckons me into his cubicle.

Oh shit.

'Have a seat, Marco.' He nods towards a chair without looking me in the face. 'We've got a problem.'

'Yeah, sorry about yesterday. I had to go home and check on my dad.'

'That's not what I want to talk about. You haven't had a sale in ages, so I have to give your region to someone else.'

'What? It's just a bad month. It'll pick up.'

'Yeah, I don't think so. It's been a long time. You can work till the end of the week, which will give you time to hand over the paperwork. I'll pay you for the month. The others aren't doing great, but they're at least making a few sales.'

'What do you mean, Owen? I've outperformed all of those idiots.'

'Maybe at one time you did. I can't afford to keep you. I'm sorry, but it's business. It's you or me.'

'Ohh. Fuck.'

I leave his cubicle and have to walk past Derek and the rest of the staff in the open-plan office; everyone would have heard our conversation. I don't even bother looking at Derek, but I imagine the smug look on his ugly face. He knows he's about to get my region.

I grab a folder from a filing cabinet and head out the door with it tucked under my arm. They can find their own fuckin' clients. I walk to McGinty's, five minutes away. The tiny Irish pub is squashed between two restaurants. The wooden bar just inside the entranceway stretches all the way to the dimly lit area at the back. I order a double bourbon and coke with no ice and slide into one of the grimy booths. I down the drink and order another two. I wait for the alcohol to make me feel better, but it's going to take a few.

I sidle home and traipse up the three flights of stairs to my apartment. My key won't open the door. I peer more closely and see that the prick's changed the lock. Fuck. I told him I'd pay him by the end of the week. I pick up the mail outside my door and shuffle through the envelopes. Bill, bill, bill. I toss them to the ground.

There's a handwritten note from the cock.

You get your stuff when I get my money.

I slide down onto the floor and thump the back of my head against the door. I just can't get a break. The old bird from across the hallway opens her door and peers out. She frowns as she sees me sitting on the floor.

'Piss off!'

'Ooh,' she says as she pops back into her apartment.

I sigh as I thrust myself up. *What a fuckin' mess.*

I walk down to the landlord's flat on the ground floor. I'd gladly walk away without paying him, but some of my designer suits are worth a lot more than the rent. The lousy prick couldn't wait a few weeks for things to get sorted, and yet I had to wait a month for him to fix a dripping tap. My stomach actually cramps as I count the money into his hand. I clench my fists beside me as he makes a production of counting it out again.

'This just brings you up to date. I'll need another two weeks' rent in advance.'

'I don't have that at the moment. I'll get it to you soon.'

'We're done playing that game. If you don't have it now, you can get your stuff and go.'

I follow him back up the stairs. He stands guard by the door as I throw my few things into a suitcase. I toss my bag into the back of my car and screech out of the basement carpark. At least I have the satisfaction of knowing that the next time he takes his prized Audi out, he'll have a key scratch along his passenger door to remember me by.

A neon bar sign calls out to me on the fringe of the city, and I pull in and park. I order a Jack Daniel's with no ice and slug it back. I tip out the change in my pocket. After paying for the drink, I'm left with a pound to my name.

The fuel indicator light comes on as soon as I get back on the M1. I gaze straight ahead and pretend for a moment that I'm free to keep driving. Then I indicate left at the last minute and take the turn-off for Radley.

JAMES

'You need to let some fresh air in here, James.' Mum pushes the window open as wide as it will go, but the air remains hot and still. I pick a book up from the bedside table and pretend to read, but the words swim on the page, and I don't absorb any of them.

Mum moves around my room slowly. Hovering. Picking up folded clothes from a chair and moving them to rest on top of my tallboy. I keep the book at face height as a barrier between us. I have no words to explain to her about the fire that's raging in my brain, or that I think my brain may explode at any moment. Even the thought of forming words is exhausting. I try to concentrate on the pressure at the back of my head where it rests on the pillow.

I feel her sit down on the end of my bed.

'Can I get you anything from town, James?'

'I'm okay.'

'What about some fruit?'

'No.'

'A magazine?'

'No. I don't need anything other than to be left alone.'

She sighs and pushes herself up. I see the sag in her shoulders and instantly regret my words.

'I just need to rest, Mum.' My tired is unlike any other tired I've known. It's a physical and mental lethargy that makes getting out of bed seem like an insurmountable task. No one could possibly understand this. Every day I hope that I'll wake up and feel normal, and yet each day that state seems further away.

'Maybe you can rest this morning and then take a walk to the library this afternoon. I have to go to the city with your dad, but I have a stack of books that need returning. Can you please do that for me, James?'

'Sure.' I turn towards the wall so I don't have to see her face. It's enough coping with my own pain.

EMILY

I tilt my face up to the shower head and let the hot water rain down on me. The cascading water helps me to think and washes away my tears. I touch the tender part on the inside of my thigh. All I ever wanted was to be someone's wife. I want so much to stay married, but I don't think I can. I step from the shower. Although the mirror is half fogged up, I see the dark purple colouring at the top of my arms. Something has to change. I just need to open my mouth and say what needs to be said. I have to pick my moment. I pull on a long-sleeved jersey and rub some concealer on the dark shades beneath my eyes. I need to do it tonight.

I miss having Colleen to talk to. Until I got married, she was like my mum and my best friend rolled up in one. I could talk to her about anything, and she always knew what to say to make me feel better—but this is different. I already know what she'll say about Rob. She's told me that she doesn't trust him or believe he has any nice qualities. Yesterday, she had a problem with the way his upper lip stretched tight across his top teeth. She said it was a sure sign of meanness. I told her that was definitely the pot calling the kettle black.

I tuck my bag under the front desk at work. I gather up the book-covering roll and our library stamp from one of the cupboards.

'I'll make a start on covering these children's books,' I call out. I take the stuff to a corner table. Colleen drops her bag beside mine, grabs a pile of books and joins me at the table. She's quiet for about a minute.

'If I can do something, I'd like to,' Colleen says.

'Yeah, you can do the stamping.'

'I don't mean that.'

I lower my head. I have to squint to check that I've placed the book exactly in the middle of the covering. I use an old duster to squash out creases and air bubbles. When I'm finished with the front, I flip the book over and do the same on the back.

I can still feel Colleen looking at me.

'I'm fine.'

'Okay. When you decide that you're not, let me know.'

She bangs the stamp on the inside of the book and claps the book shut, then picks up another. I'm saved from any more comments by Mrs Ester— Mrs Wildfire if her back is turned. If there is anything you want spread around the village, she's the lady you go to.

'What's happening about that documentary, Mrs Ester?' I ask, knowing that I'll get more than the full story.

'You'll never believe it, Emily, but they've put a chair in the square.'

'What?'

'A chair, Emily. They've built a little shelter up in the market square and put a chair in there.'

'What for?'

'As well as walking around and filming us, they've got some fancy camera that people can turn on and film themselves with. Annie says it's some sort of reality show about life in a village, but I've got no idea what she's talking about. I think they're having another meeting tonight. In here, isn't it, Colleen?'

'Yes, just after the church meeting. It starts at seven.'

Mrs Ester nods and walks towards the romance section. Several people come in at once, so I gather up the stuff on the table and return it to the cupboard.

Colleen places some new releases on a stand at the front of the library. We have a mountain of returned books; I sort them alphabetically before placing them on the trolley. As I wheel it down one of the rows, I hear Mrs Ester's high-pitched voice again. For a moment, I don't know who she's talking to.

'Did you hear about William?' she asks.

'No, what's happened?' I crane my neck to see who she's talking to. Ah—it's Mrs Ashby.

'I heard that he isn't who he said he was.'

'What do you mean?'

'Well, apparently, the surname we know him by is different to the name on his NHS card.'

'Who told you that?'

'Myrtle did.'

'How would she know anything?'

'Her daughter works at the doctor's. Didn't I say that there was something fishy about him? That he was hiding from something.'

'He's been here for twenty years, Ina.'

'Well, years don't lessen people's crimes. I heard that he was involved with a minor.'

'That's just village gossip.'

'Well, I wouldn't be surprised. Just look at the way he dresses—and the way he hangs around our Emily.'

I step from behind the shelves. 'Can I help you two find something?' They both look surprised, and I'm happy to see that at least Mrs Ashby looks embarrassed to be caught gossiping.

'No, just found it.' Mrs Ester grabs a book from the display shelf and moves off.

I have to wait a moment for the shaking in my hands to subside before I follow her to the counter. 'People need to check their facts before they spread rumours,' I say as I scan the barcodes and thump her books into a pile.

'I'm just passing on what I heard, Emily.' She stuffs her books into her bag and marches out of the library.

WILLIAM

A ferocious wind came unannounced and uprooted trees and took down our power lines. I watch from my window seat as it rips the last of the leaves from the branches and hurls them to the ground. Juno whimpers and cowers until I feel sorry for her and bring her bed in from the porch. Arlo brought over a camp stove and some candles. He told me that the main road out of town is blocked by a fallen oak.

There's something comforting about being trapped indoors while a storm whips around. There's a buffer between you and the 'real world'. But then, the real world has a way of catching up with you. Radley's been my cabin in the woods for so long now that I'd almost forgotten that I was once another William.

I spend the day indoors, but at four I wander to the library.

I can hear the sound from inside before I push open the doors. Children are strewn everywhere; they cascade down the stairs from the rooms above. The smell from the kerosene lamps fills the air, and the AGA in the kitchen and the gas heaters warm the entire space. I turn to leave, but Colleen waves me in. Emily looks up and attempts a smile from her seat on the floor. I notice the dark circles under her eyes. Expectant faces gaze up at her as she reads from an oversized picture book.

'And then when all the honey jars were empty, the bear jumped out of the window and ran straight into the woods.'

'Your books are on the second shelf under the desk, William. Help yourself,' Colleen calls out over the noise.

I find the books. As I pick them up, I see the boy from the bridge reading in one of the alcoves. I think of going to say hello, but the noise down here is too much. As I walk past the children, one of the parents grabs a child's hand and pulls her away from me. The child looks startled. I pretend I didn't see what happened.

I climb the stairs and settle in a wing-back chair in one of the back bedrooms. I try to read, but I keep reading the same line as my mind wanders back to the mother's reaction. It's human nature to judge people by the way they look, and usually I pay it no mind, but some days that stuff gets in.

Rather than follow the thought too far down the rabbit hole, I pull the notepad and pen from my coat. I don't know how people make sense of the world without writing it out.

I find company in the flawed protagonists who live between the pages of books. They offer me something to hold on to. There's a sliver of hope that we can leave our pasts behind and maybe even find forgiveness.

I write until the light moves to another part of the library. I'm about to follow the light when the power comes back on. A cacophony of voices and people moving fills the air. I wait until the racket subsides and slowly wander home.

I grab some more wood and stoke the fire as soon as I'm home. I hear a slight tap, and then Arlo walks in.

'William? Oh good, you're home. How you doing?'

'Pretty good. Do you want a cuppa?'

'No. I just wanted to see how you are. I saw Bernie up the street, and she said you didn't look good.'

'I'm fine. You know her. She's had me dying since the day I moved in here.'

We both laugh, but I can see Arlo checking me out.

'I've changed my mind about a cuppa. I'll make it.' He strolls into the kitchen. 'Do you want one?'

'Yes, a peppermint would be nice. How's Marco?' I ask, signalling for a change of subject.

'Still the same. A shit. I swear he gets more like his mother every day. I should tell him, and he might stop hating her so much.' He clatters around in the kitchen and comes back a few minutes later.

He places my tea on a small side table and drags an armchair closer to me. A frown creases his brow.

'He'll be alright, Arlo.'

'Yeah, that's what you've been telling me for years. But I think the fruit is spoiled.'

I smile at my friend's use of English. He loves telling people that he took to proverbs and clichés like a duck to water.

'He needs some of that pie that you Englishmen eat,' Arlo says.

'What pie?'

'You know, the one you eat when you've grown too big for yourself.'

'Oh, humble.'

'Yeah. He needs a big slice of that.'

'He's still growing up.'

'He's thirty, William. He's not a boy.'

'It takes a long time to grow up, Arlo.'

Arlo sips his tea and nods his head. 'I suppose I should be grateful. At least he's not crashing cars and getting into fights any more.'

'He was just mad that his mum left. People do funny things when they're hurting.'

'Yeah, I think he's still making people pay for that.'

We hear a car in Arlo's driveway. He stands up and looks out the window.

'Talk of the devil. I'd better go see what he wants from me now.'

'I've got a few jobs I need doing. Send him over here when he's got a minute.'

'My pleasure.'

MARCO

Dad walks through the gap in the hedge from William's garden as I'm taking my suitcases from the car.

'Marco. Twice in one week. I didn't expect to see you for another year.'

'Yeah, well. I lost my job. The boss turned out to be a dick.'

'You have an uncanny knack for finding one of those for a boss.'

'Funny, Dad. I thought I'd stay here until I can sort some things out.'

'Right.'

He takes one of my suitcases from me, and I follow him inside. I'm surprised he's not giving me more grief. I search his face to see what's going on.

'Are you okay?'

'Yeah, bit worried about William.'

'It was just a cut.'

'Mmm. Think it's a bit more than that. He said they're going to run a few tests at the hospital, but he's not saying much more. I did offer to drive him, but he said he'd catch the train. Maybe you could go over and convince him to take a ride? You could pretend you're going back to London for the day. He'd probably go with you.'

'He'll be fine, Dad. It's William. Anyway, I'm busy looking for a job.'

'William's not invincible, Marco. You can spend your time at the hospital checking the newspaper.'

'You don't get jobs through newspapers any more. They're online.'

'Well, that's even better. You're always on your phone; you'll get one in no time. I've got a huge delivery, and that film crew coming to get some things from the shop. It'll help me out if you can take him.'

'What time is it?'

'I think his appointment's at 1 p.m. He won't mind waiting if you need to do some stuff afterwards.'

I frown at the thought of taking William to a bar, which is the only thing I'm interested in doing.

'What if they tell him something horrible? Maybe you should come too. In case he wants to talk about it or something?'

'You'll be fine. It'll be nice for him to have you there. Payback for all the times he's been there for you.'

I grab my bags from the floor, and memories of William saving my arse flood in.

'Yeah, yeah. I'll do it.' I throw my bags into my old room. The childish cowboy curtains that Dad got cheap when I was already too old for them hang limp from the windows. I put my suits in the wardrobe, but the pole is at kids' height, and they drag on the floor. I place my dress shoes on top of the bookshelves, which are made from planks of wood and concrete blocks. Dad was so excited about his creation that most of our rooms have at least one set of them. I sink down onto my single bed, and a spring pokes through the worn mattress and jabs me in the rear.

JAMES

'I got interviewed by that film crew today,' Mum says as she brings a fish pie to the table. 'I made your favourite, James.'

Tonight, the smell of it makes me nauseous, and I hide my gagging behind a napkin. I feel sick in my stomach a lot of the time. There's a constant rumbling and churning going on inside. I take a sip of water and hope it stays down.

'Where did you see the film crew?' Dad asks.

'At the butcher's. I was getting some meat, and they were in there interviewing Earl and Rose.'

'I would have thought they'd start further up the chain than them.'

'They had to start somewhere. Their shop's the first on Spring Street. I'm sure they'll get to you soon.'

'I should think so. Actually, I'm glad they didn't come into the office today, because the only thing people wanted to talk about was the manse being sold and the library shutting down.'

'It's a big deal, Raymond,' Mum says. 'Loads of groups use that library.'

'Well, they'll just have to go somewhere else. What did the film crew ask you?'

'How long I'd been here. What it's like living in a small village.'

'Did you tell them you're married to the clerk of the parish council?'

'No. They didn't ask that sort of thing.'

'You don't need to be asked. The only way for me to get elected to the county council is for us to take every opportunity to promote what I do on the parish council.'

The air seems compressed, and it feels like the roof is pressing down on us as they're talking. I glance up at the ceiling and then at Mum to see if she's noticing it as well. She smiles and seems oblivious.

I force down a mouthful. One more and I'll throw up. I put my knife and fork together. 'I'm sorry, Mum, but I'm not really hungry.'

'Do you want me to make you a …'

'Oh, for God's sake, Marion. Stop mollycoddling the boy.' Dad slaps some butter on a chunk of bread and stuffs it in his mouth. He chews it without taking his eyes off me.

'Have you decided on a plan yet, James?'

'I haven't had much time to think.'

'Mmm. Seems to me that you've got all the time in the world.'

Mum doesn't look up from her plate.

'Well, I don't think it's good for you to be lying around the house all day, so you can come and work at the office with me. I've got a few jobs on the computer that need doing. Lindy can set you up out the back.'

'I'm not really that good on a computer.'

'See, even that's strange.' He directs his words towards Mum and then turns back towards me. 'You must be the only kid this century who doesn't understand technology.'

'I understand it, Dad. I'm just not into it.'

He shakes his head like he doesn't know what to think.

'Can we leave it for the moment, Raymond?'

'I'm just trying to find a solution. Maybe you can ask around the village to see if there's a part-time job until we get you into another university.'

'I'm not sure that's what I want to do.'

'Oh ... Well, the one thing I am sure of is that you're not going to find the answer you're looking for in your bedroom. You have to get out more. It might seem to you that I'm being cruel, but I think you'll thank me for it in the end.'

EMILY

Colleen watches me as I put books into the wrong places. I have to keep saying the alphabet out loud because I can't remember what letter comes next.

'Oh, for God's sake, Emily. Do some dusting.' She thrusts a cloth into my hand. 'I don't have time for this today. What's going on?'

'Nothing, I'm just tired.'

'You look awful. Maybe you should take a few days off.'

'No. I don't need to.'

'It's not just me who thinks you look dreadful. Other people are starting to comment.'

'People. You mean Maggie?'

'No, not just Maggie. Lots of people.'

'Well, you can tell "lots of people" to mind their own business.'

'Emily, I'm concerned.'

'I told you that I haven't been sleeping well. I'll come right.'

'That's what I've been waiting for, but it doesn't appear to be happening.'

I can see by the look in her eyes and the way her mouth is set that she won't let this go.

'You're right. I probably need some vitamins.' I march off before she can say anything more. I know that I'm about a millisecond away from coming undone.

I don't understand how it all turned so horrible. Last night I made a beautiful beef stew with dumplings and waited until he'd eaten his dinner. I served him up a huge slice of lemon meringue pie before I said anything. It took me all my courage to open my mouth and get the words out—that I wasn't happy with the way he was treating me.

I can't believe I was so stupid.

The look of anger that spread across his face was so quick that I didn't have time to move. I knew I was in trouble. He leapt around the table and shoved me against the wall. He spat words at me, but I was so frightened that I couldn't make any sense of them. I thought he was going to hit me, but instead he punched a hole in the wall beside my head. I felt the pee dribble down my leg as he released his grip. He stormed upstairs to bed, and I waited until

I could hear him snore before grabbing some clothes and walking through the dark to the library.

I woke in the bedroom off the kitchen. The French doors lead out to a small potager. Since I was a child, this has always been my favourite room. It took me a few moments to remember why I was here, but then the memories came flooding back. I sat on the edge of the bed and felt like crying, but no tears came. Perhaps you run out of them. I made the bed and hid my clothes and toiletries under the stairs before Colleen arrived.

Beatrice bustles in not long after we open, and Colleen surprises me by blocking the entrance to the kitchen.

'I think it's time, Beatrice, that you got your coffee somewhere else.'

'You're being petty, Colleen. This wasn't just my decision.'

'Maybe not, but you were the driving force behind it. I saw that first-hand at the meeting. If the library has to move, then I see no reason for us to put up with you a minute longer.'

'This is a public library, Colleen.'

'Yes, it is. So if you want to borrow a book, be my guest, but if you're wanting coffee, I suggest you go to the highway tearooms and pay like everyone else.'

'What do you mean, if the library has to move?' I ask.

Colleen swivels around to face me and looks uncomfortable.

'I'll explain later, Emily.'

'There's not much to explain, Colleen,' Beatrice says through gritted teeth. She turns towards me. 'The church needs urgent repairs, Emily, or we won't have a church. We have to sell the manse to pay for this. The library will need to be rehoused.'

'But ... where will I go?'

WILLIAM

I heard it once, but I replay the diagnosis throughout the day. Two big growths, inoperable, but treatments may help. Having had a feeling that something was wrong doesn't make knowing any easier. Some things are just too big to absorb at once. They have to sit somewhere until you can work out how to break them down into smaller chunks. Words that I've known forever have been tipped on their heads and sound different. 'Treatments', 'options', 'most likely'.

I can feel the pressure behind my eyes. I sit down on the window seat and prop some cushions behind my back. I thought the day would come when my past would catch up with me, but I never imagined that a cluster of cells that refuse to die like they're supposed to would steal the limelight. Take away my options.

Juno starts barking. Out the window, I see a policeman weaving his way through my garden.

I open the door before he reaches it.

'Good afternoon,' I call out.

He nods in my direction and walks slowly up the path and onto the porch.

'I'm Sergeant Norris,' he says as he steps around me and into my lounge. His head starts rotating. He reminds me of the fairground clowns, the ones who turn their heads as you try to put the ball in their mouths.

'Can I help you with something?'

He doesn't answer for a moment but continues to move his head. He looks at me, and I sense that he doesn't like me.

'I'm the new sergeant. I've taken over from Sergeant Goff. I'd like to take a look inside your shed.'

'Can I ask what you're looking for?'

'We're concerned that you might be operating something illegally from your shed. We've had quite a few reports about people coming and going from your property. I'm here to take a look around.'

'And if I wouldn't like to show you?'

'I'll look anyway.'

His smile is full of menace. I shake my head, but I know that arguing will keep him here longer. I take the key from a hook and point towards the shed. Juno growls as he walks past her. He strides off down the path like he's on a treasure hunt. I'm not sure what he's expecting to find. Bodies? Or parts of them?

I open the door and hold a hand out, indicating he should go in first. The smell of white sage and juniper hangs in the air. He sniffs loudly as he stoops to get inside. He looks at the books on the shelves. I see him reading the quotes that I've painted in gold around the walls. He sits down in one of the two armchairs that face each other and shuffles through the books on the coffee table. 'Forest bathing. Bringing yoga to life …' He snorts and shakes his head as he stands. He pulls a few more books from the shelves. His shoulders sag, and I sense his disappointment. I think he was hoping for a magic lever or a trapdoor.

'So you're selling books, are you?'

'No.'

'So what are these all for?'

I look at him. 'Really. You want me to answer that?'

'I want you to answer all my questions.' He pulls himself up to maximum height.

'They're for reading.'

He pulls his lips tightly together. 'I can take you down to the station, William.'

'On what grounds?'

'On the grounds that I'm a police officer.'

'Mmm. I think you'll need a bit more than that.'

'On the grounds, William, that I believe you may be engaging in several criminal activities.'

'Perhaps you'd like to name one.'

'Child grooming. Drug manufacturing.'

'That's ridiculous.'

'You've been seen dropping things off around the village, and I hear that people visit you in this shed.'

'I don't think that's a crime. Unless you've got a warrant, get off my property.' I turn and walk towards the house. Juno barks at him and follows me up the path.

'I'll be back, William,' he calls out from the gate.

I am shaking. I slouch down in the nearest chair and inhale through my nose to the count of three, then exhale to the same count. I repeat this until my body relaxes.

I hear a knock on the door and then Arlo calling out to me.

'Are you alright, William?'

'Yes. I'm fine.'

'I just saw a policeman leaving your house. I thought I'd better see what trouble you've been getting into.'

'He's new. He's just checking me out.'

'Why?'

'He would have heard the rumours and decided to pay me a visit. He's just trying to make a good impression.'

'I don't know why you don't put the record straight, William.'

'It's no business of mine what other people think of me.'

'But you know it's all twisted and made up. They say you've done heinous things.'

'I have done heinous things, Arlo.'

'In your mind. Anyway, we're talking about a long time ago, William.'

I look out to the garden and push open the window, and a warm breeze wafts in. The leaves of the horse chestnut are just starting to change from saffron to a deep red. I'll miss watching the leaves unfurling like a giant's fingers in early spring.

'Who do you think forgives you, Arlo? If you don't believe in a God?'

'I don't know. Maybe you forgive yourself. Forgiveness doesn't turn a wrong into a right, William. It just means that you accept that what was done has been done.' He raises his eyebrows at me like he's asked a question and is waiting for an answer.

MARCO

'There's no way I'm working at the gala, Dad.'

'Don't be mean, Marco. It's a fundraiser for the kids.'

'I'm not being mean. I'm not Florence fuckin' Nightingale. I took William to the hospital yesterday. I don't need to do a gala day as well.'

'It's not about need, Marco. You love William. And anyway, this is your village. Why wouldn't you want to help?'

'Because it's a stupid village, Dad. Everyone's all up in everyone's shit.'

'It'll do you good to get involved in your community. You might even learn something. Anyway, what sort of business are you doing that you'd care if people knew?'

'Have you finished?'

'Actually, no, I haven't. You're on dinner—and I already told them you'd help. Think of it as paying your board.'

I feel like throwing something at him as he walks away.

'When is it?' I yell at his back.

'Tomorrow, so you can help me in the garden today.'

I spend the afternoon digging another plot for him, although he already grows way too many vegetables. He wanders around the village like Friar Tuck, leaving little boxes of his surplus veggies on people's doorsteps.

I stack concrete blocks around the back of his shed. I think he might have some hoarding tendencies—nothing gets thrown out. I sort onions, garlic and beets on an old filleting bench at the back of the garden. I see my penknife skills along one side: *Marco was here and then he left! 2000*. I grab a Stanley knife from the shed and slice *Left forever 2020* underneath it.

In the morning, I see Dad checking out what I'm wearing.

'I thought you were helping me at the gala.'

'I am.'

'Oh. Nice of you to dress up for us.'

'I like to make a good impression. Just because I come from a village doesn't mean I have to dress like it.'

'Suit yourself.' He smiles at his pun.

They've got the same stupid fête flag outside the office that they used when I was at school. Throngs of people are already crowding the gates. I tilt my head down as we drive through the main entrance to unload the vegetables. I help Dad move the heavy bags into a classroom. We have to make several trips. He wanders off halfway through unloading. A balding man in jeans that are too tight in the crotch steers himself towards me. He looks like the sort of guy who could carry on a conversation about nothing all day. Hoping to avoid him, I scan the crowd for Dad and spot him talking to an attractive woman over by some sheep. I wander over and give him a look that I hope conveys my unhappiness at being here.

'Marco, this is Philippa Seymour. She's the new headmistress here.'

I can't help but notice that Ms Headmistress has amazing legs.

'I might have stayed at school longer if we'd had teachers like you.'

She doesn't return my smile but puts out her hand for me to shake.

'Nice to meet you, Marco. Your dad helps us out a lot.'

'Yeah, I think he's after an OBE.'

'He might get one. Thanks for helping us out too. It was hard finding an auctioneer at such short notice.'

I look at Dad, but he turns away and is suddenly very interested in the sheep.

'Um. I don't think so, Philippa. I don't know anything about that.'

Philippa looks confused.

Dad grimaces.

'Sorry, I didn't get a chance to tell you,' he says. 'Reg pulled out at the last minute, so I thought, you know, you being top salesman in London, you'd be perfect. Look how nice you're dressed too.' Dad grins.

'We really appreciate it.' Now Philippa gives me a smile. 'It's raffles, so you're not really auctioning anything, just calling out the prizes.'

I look again at her legs and up to her boobs. No wedding ring on her finger.

'Yeah, okay.'

'Great. Come on, I'll take you over to the truck.'

'A truck?'

'Mmm, that's our stage. You'll be on the back of it.'

Dad smiles at me and walks away. I hear him say, 'A rock and a hard place'.

I stare at the back of his head.

'So how long have you been in the village?' I ask her.

'I started at the beginning of the term.'

'Hope the townsfolk haven't been too cruel. Teachers usually fare better than most, at least. So, you would have been subjected to the village inquisition?'

'Oh yes, I've been interrogated by the butcher, the baker and the candlestick maker. Or at least their wives. I think I may have fallen short of a pass as I'm missing a spouse. Your dad said top salesman. What did you sell?'

'Apartments in central London.' I push up the sleeve of my suit to expose my Rolex. 'I'm just having a break at the moment.'

She nods without looking at me or the watch and waves to someone.

'I'd better go and check up on a few things. Wait here, and I'll send someone over to help you. I'll give them the list of what we're selling. They'll hold up the item and deal with the money side. Thanks again.'

I watch her arse as she walks away. I'm thinking that a few hours on the back of a truck is a fair trade for a piece of that.

A few minutes later, I hear a familiar high-pitched voice. I turn around, and Kay Baxter is rushing towards me, waving sheets of paper in the air.

'I'm your assistant, Marco,' she squawks from across the field.

JAMES

Every morning, Mum comes in and opens my curtains to let the light in, yet every day, I feel the darkness creep a little closer. This morning I get up before her. I drag yesterday's clothes from the floor and pull them on, then stuff a T-shirt into a backpack. I take my coat from the hook by the door, and I'm halfway out it when Mum walks into the hallway.

'Where are you going, James? It's not even light outside.'

'I'm going for a walk and then maybe to the library when it opens. You can tell Dad I've gone to look for a job.'

The path to the river is deserted, and I head towards the old railway bridge. I traverse the track under it and hide myself behind one of the concrete pylons, covered in years of graffiti. An odour of decay rises up from the ground.

A big boulder obscures the path below me. I put my coat down on the damp grass and use the T-shirt I brought as a pillow. I lie down on top of the bag and close my eyes. It's hard for me to sleep, but it's harder to be awake. I count out loud in the hope of drowning out the voice in my head.

'Hello.'

I sit bolt upright and turn towards the voice. William and Juno stand at the top of the bank. William slides down and stumbles to a stop. Juno snips and snaps her body around the boulders and bounds up to me like we're lifelong friends. She licks me and then picks up my backpack with her mouth. She drags it towards William and leaves it on the grass between us.

'I'm sorry,' he says. 'I think she may have been a packhorse in a previous life, as she loves carrying things.'

Juno comes back to me and plonks herself alongside me. She rests one of her paws on my leg. William follows Juno's tracks, and then he too sits down beside me. I wait for him to speak, but he doesn't. He just sits there, gazing out across the river below.

I look at the dog and the old man sitting next to me. My thoughts scream at him, *What are you doing? Go away.* I say nothing. William turns his face towards the sky. 'That breeze feels so good on my face.' He tilts his chin upwards and closes his eyes and appears to go to sleep. I keep staring at him. Willing him to go away.

'Have you read any of Kierkegaard's writing, James?'

I don't answer. My brain is trying to process what's happening. I don't even know this man.

'He said that life can only be understood backwards; but we have to live it forwards first. I think that's one of the most profound things I've ever heard.'

He stares at me, and then he flinches. I get a fright when Juno leaps up and bounds over to William. She nudges his arm and then goes around to his other side. With her nose, she urges him to get up. As he stands, I see him wince with pain.

'Ooh, that was nasty. I think Juno's telling me it's time to get home.'

I look at the dog and then back at William.

'Are you alright?'

'Mmm, I will be. I know it's an imposition, but would you mind walking a little way with us? I have a bit of a headache, which is affecting my sight. I'm just on Spring Street.'

I want to say no, but the sky is only just starting to lighten, and there is no one else around. I nod and help William up the bank. Juno leads, and it only takes a few minutes before we're at his house.

I think everyone in the village knows where he lives. A lot of people in Radley can trace their family here back five generations. They've never taken kindly to strangers. Especially dishevelled ones who don't go to church. I've seen kids from the village throwing food and obscenities his way. I remember seeing him up a ladder on my way home from school once. Classical music blared from speakers on his porch, and he appeared happy as he hosed off ugly words that had been painted on his house.

William leans over and unlatches the willow gate.

'Thanks, James.'

'Will you be alright?'

'Yeah, I'll be fine.'

I watch him as he turns away. He only manages a few steps, and then he appears to slump. Juno turns and barks at me.

'Do you want some help?'

He just nods his head.

I take him inside, and he falls into a chair.

'Shall I ring someone?'

'No, I'll come right in a minute, and I've got Juno. I just overdid our walk. Would you mind moving that stuff off there for me?'

I move the cushions to one end of the sofa. I gather up the newspaper and a few books and place them on the floor.

He stumbles over and lies down.

'Thanks, James. I'll be good now.' He pretends to smile.

Juno licks my hand on her way past to lie alongside the sofa.

EMILY

I tuck my small canvas bag of overnight things into the cupboard under the cedar stairs. It's more like a room than a cupboard and has an armchair by the window. You can walk around easily without banging your head on the stairs. A yellow stained-glass window lets the light in, and even when the sun's not shining outside, in here it feels like it is. I wonder how much longer I'll have the refuge of the library.

I can't even imagine my life without the manse in it. Where would I go every day, for a start? I know Colleen is suspicious that I'm sleeping over. I'm thankful that she's preoccupied and hasn't said anything. Everything seems wrong, and I don't know how to make it right. I feel anxious, and I don't trust myself to make the right decisions about anything. It's just like it was when my grandmother was alive. Throwing dirt onto the top of her coffin was one of my happiest moments. Today, I'd get pleasure from throwing dirt onto the top of Rob's coffin as well. I know that makes me a horrible wife and an awful person, but it's the truth.

I shouldn't have read so many romance novels—then perhaps I wouldn't have had such a ridiculous idea about love. I thought being married would make everything better, not worse. The longer I'm married to him, the more he drinks and the worse his temper gets. I stay out of his way as much as possible, but I have a knack of winding him up. My grandmother's voice screams inside my head. *It's your own fault, Emily. If you weren't so stupid, I wouldn't get so mad.* I suppose I have her to thank for making me good at reading people's faces. As soon as I see the skin above Rob's mouth draw tight, I know it's time to leave. If I can make it out the front door, then I'm safe. There's no way he'd bother to come look for me.

I know what Maggie was suggesting when she said that Rob had been seen hanging around the fish 'n' chip shop. Everyone knows that Lindy at the chippy will give you more than a free packet of sauce. I wanted to tell her that I'd already worked that out by myself, but I played dumb. When Rob came home last week, he had a strange smell about him. I was in the post office the next day and got a waft of the same scent. I turned around and saw Lindy, and it dawned on me in a rush. Cheap perfume, mixed with fat from the fryers. That's why he's been leaving me alone. I know everyone in the village will be feeling sorry for me, but I want to send her a thank-you card.

On my way home, I see William in his back garden chopping the deadheads off a flowering shrub. He waves and smiles when he sees me.

'Hi, William.'

'Hi, Emily. Have you got time for tea?'

I look at my watch. Rob's not due home for an hour, and I only have to warm up his dinner.

'I'll have a quick one. Thanks.'

He puts the secateurs into a jacket pocket, and I follow him down the winding path to his garden shed. I choose the frayed armchair closest to the door and collapse into it. He brews a pot of tea and places it like a peace offering on the coffee table between us. I pour some milk into a cup and add a teaspoon of sugar. I look around at his books lining the shelves. Any empty wall space has been painted with phrases, and even the back of the door has *One day at a time* written on it in large letters.

He swipes at his brow and pulls a strand of long grey hair off his face.

'What's happening, Emily?'

'What do you mean?'

'I mean, how are you?'

'I'm okay.'

He holds both his hands around his teacup and takes a deliberate long sip. He looks at me across the rim, and I feel the tears welling up.

'Take your time, Emily. I wasn't a good doctor, but I am a good listener.'

Instead of taking just one breath in, I inhale three times.

'I don't think I can stay married.'

'Oh.'

'I don't think he loves me.' I bite my bottom lip and keep staring at the ground. 'I can't seem to do anything right. I thought ... if I just tried harder, I could make it work ... but I can't try any harder. I can't make him happy.'

'I don't think it's our job to make other people happy.'

'That's what wives are supposed to do.'

He shakes his head. 'I think it's more likely that we're in charge of our own happiness.'

I shrug my shoulders and let out a huge sigh.

'I made a promise in a church: "till death do us part". I want to keep that promise.'

'Sometimes promises get broken.'

'My grandmother always said that if I did manage to find a husband, he wouldn't stay with me long. I hate that she might get to be right.'

'She's not right. And she's not here. You don't need to listen to that voice any more.'

'I don't know what to do. My thoughts are all over the place.'

'What's your heart telling you to do?'

'It's telling me to leave, but it's the same heart that told me I was in love and I should get married. I'm not sure I trust it.'

'Trust yourself, Emily. You're the only one who can make this decision, but it's obvious that you're not happy. Something needs to change.'

'That's what Colleen says as well. The bit about me not being happy.' I sit up straight in my chair. 'You can't tell Colleen about this, William, until I work out what to do. She already thinks I'm stupid for marrying him.'

'She won't think you're stupid, Emily. She cares about you. There are a lot of people in this village who care about you, Emily.'

I lean forward, and the clock above his head chimes six.

'God, I've got to go.'

WILLIAM

I wake with a stiffness in my neck and the now familiar ache in my temple. I close my eyes and take a big breath in and then a long exhalation. I visualise the pain being taken away on the out-breath. I breathe in and out ten more times before opening my eyes again. It seems that there will be no getting away from the pain this morning. The oncologist said that as the tumour grew, it would become more painful and slowly start to affect my mobility. Yesterday, I stumbled twice, and the third time I fell over onto the gravel. I had hoped for a little more time.

I've never been a great keeper of time, but now that I'm running out of it, it does seem important to spend it wisely. I sense an urgency from somewhere to put things right. To put things in order is really what I mean. Some things can never be put right.

I slide the metal box from under the window seat and take the letters out. I read the faded address, although I know it by heart. All the letters I wrote, put in an envelope and addressed but never sent. There was always such a distance between the thoughts in my head and the words that came out on paper. I thought for a while that what I had to say might be better to say in person, but I haven't been brave enough yet.

I take pen and paper and stare into space, hoping to find words that convey my thoughts. I stall on the starting line. How do you start a letter to someone knowing that you altered the whole course of their life? I try again and then scribble across what I've written. I tear off a clean sheet and force myself to write.

It is hard to find the words to explain what's in my thoughts, and I hope that the ones I choose don't upset you. There appears to be no bigger word than sorry, so that is all I can offer.

I hear a thump on the outside of my house; I'm grateful for the interruption. I put my latest offering on top of the others in the box and slide it back under the window seat.

MARCO

Dad's shop sits at the bottom of High Street in an old wool warehouse. It's the perfect spot for catching the tourists as they do the loop around town. I unlock the brass padlock and slide the bolt back. I'm breaking my vow to never work in the shop again, because I can't watch William being poked and prodded at the hospital.

This warehouse used to house the wool bales before they got taken to the mill. The chunky beams overhead form a peak and make the roof seem miles away, like you're in a cathedral. The dark stained floorboards are replicated in the mezzanine that juts out over half the shop. Some of the pulley ropes still dangle from the rafters.

The notorious Finnleigh gang were said to have hidden out in the cellar of this building when one of their smuggling operations went wrong. They were eventually found hiding in the wool bales and then hanged in the market square. I used to charge the kids from my class a sherbet or a 50p bag of sweets to come have a look at where the gang had etched their names into the stonework while they hid from the customs agents. Dad put a stop to it when he realised what I was doing. He made it known that locals were welcome to have a look around for free and offered me as their guide.

I open the shop at ten, and at five past, the Driscoll clan traipses in. Mr and Mrs My Shit Doesn't Stink and Clive, their entitled, pain-in-the-arse son.

We started school on the same day, and our mutual hatred of each other lasted until we both left. On that first day, I thought we could be friends, but he made it clear that he wouldn't be playing with a wog.

'Have they run out of houses for you to sell in the city?' Clive says, staring straight at me.

The thought of punching him flashes through my mind, and then it's replaced by the thought of telling Dad that I punched the first customer within five minutes of opening. I keep it together by clenching and unclenching my fists under the counter.

'No, Clive. I'm helping my old man out. Were you after anything in particular?'

His mother wobbles up to the counter. 'We only come in for the vegetables.' She picks up a marrow and inspects every inch of it before placing it into her wicker basket. She does the same with a tomato, and I have to turn away. I've never understood how the Driscolls could possibly think that owning a hardware store in some backward village elevates them above anyone else. Dad's veggies are either amazing or cheap to get the Driscolls through his door.

There is no arrangement to Dad's shop. It looks like someone opened the front doors and threw in a pile of furniture—which is probably pretty close to the truth. I drag a couple of wicker chairs onto the pavement so I can move around in the shop, and within an hour I've sold them. The same thing happens when I replace them with two wooden ones. By the end of the day, I've sold a hat stand and a table lamp, and someone's put their name down on a mahogany table that I didn't discover until I moved things outside.

I call into the Swan on my way home, to celebrate. As soon as I walk in, I regret my decision. Hunched over the bar with their bum cracks showing are Graham and Mark. Two of my biggest tormentors at school. My heart races as the adrenalin surges through my blood. I look for an escape route, just like I did as a boy.

Kay Baxter is serving drinks behind the bar.

'Hi, Marco,' she calls out, which makes them turn and look my way before I have a chance to leave.

'Well, if it isn't Fidel,' Graham says, sneering and elbowing his brother.

My shoulders automatically hunch up by my ears. I'm reminded how I used to try and make myself look small in the hope that they wouldn't notice me. I quickly weigh up my options. I'm a grown man, and I'll look like an idiot if I run. I acknowledge them with a tilt of my head, and stroll to the far end of the bar. Kay walks its length to serve me.

'I didn't think you were hanging around?'

'I'm not.' I place a ten-pound note on the bar. 'Bourbon and coke, no ice.'

I feel the brothers' eyes on me and pretend to check my phone. Kay saunters off and takes forever to pour my drink. She leans over so I can see down her top as she places the drink on a coaster in front of me. I keep my head down and pretend not to notice her. I raise the glass to my lips and take a leisurely sip, although I want to down it and run.

'What are you doing back here?' Graham asks.

'Yeah, slumming it a bit, aren't ya, Marco?' They both laugh at their lame joke.

'Just got a bit of business.'

'Right. Of course you do. Big stuff, no doubt.'

I take a few more swigs of my drink and then pretend to check my phone.

'Can I shout you another one?' Kay asks as I put my empty glass on the counter.

'I'm good.'

As I walk out, one of them yells out to me. 'See you later, DW.'

It catapults me back to the school playground, where the chanting of *dumb wog* accompanied me most lunchtimes. All I ever wished for as a child was for another immigrant family to move to the village—or at least someone who was poorer than us.

Dad is sound asleep in his chair when I get home. His false teeth sit on the side table next to him. I think about waking him and telling him about the shop sales, but I'm not in the mood to talk. The joy of the sales evaporated in the pub. I hate that those arseholes made me feel small and feeble again. I've got to find a way to get out of here.

JAMES

A dark shadow appears under the bridge, and it takes a moment for me to recognise the shape of Juno. God, not again. I look up the bank and expect to see William, but I don't.

'Where's your master?'

She grabs the end of my jacket with her teeth and pulls it.

'Let it go.' I tap at her nose, but she won't let go. I have to tug hard on the jacket before it releases. She walks halfway up the bank, stops and looks back at me. When I don't move, she barks at me and then walks back down and sits in front of me.

'Go on home.'

She still doesn't move. 'Go on, Juno.'

She pats at me with one of her front paws.

'Go on, go.'

She swats at me repetitively.

'God.'

I push her sharply, and she walks up the bank. She stops at the top, turns and looks down at me and starts barking.

'Shh. Shut up, Juno.'

I shake my head and go behind the boulder. In an instant, she's back down beside me and pulling a rope from my backpack. I go to grab her, but she's too fast and races up the bank with the rope clenched in her mouth. I chase her along the path, snatching at the rope dragging behind her, but she's too quick.

When we get to William's gate, she ducks under it and leaves me standing on the other side. William's up a ladder throwing leaves out of his gutter and onto the lawn.

He turns and smiles when he sees me.

'I wondered where she'd gone. She took off when I got the ladder out. Where'd you find her?'

'Under the bridge.'

'I thought she might be there. It seems to be her favourite place at the moment.' William climbs down. A striped pyjama top is visible under his jersey.

'Thanks for bringing her back. Actually, it's good timing. I need a hand carrying something in from the garage. Would you mind, James?'

I nod and follow him around the back of his house. I shorten my step to imitate his.

In the garage, he moves boxes aside until he locates a tea chest along the back wall. We take a side each, but it's heavy, and we have to put it down several times as we carry it into his lounge. The smells of peppermint and incense fill the air.

Juno sidles up beside him. William appears to jolt backwards. I look at Juno and presume she's knocked him off balance.

'Are you alright, William?'

'Yeah. I just overdid it. I need to sit down.'

I help him into a chair.

'Sorry this is becoming a habit, James.'

'Do you need anything?'

'A cup of tea would be nice. Maybe you could have one with me. Just until my vision sorts itself. It's all a bit fuzzy at the moment. The tea is on the bench, and the mugs are in the cupboard above.'

I follow where he's pointing. Strewn along the bench are small containers and glass beakers, like in a laboratory. It takes me a while to find the pot, the tea and two clean cups. I take them into the lounge and search for somewhere to put them. The room is filled with furniture, and every surface has something on it. Books are stacked up to near toppling. Candles in saucers in various states of decline are dotted around. A coffee cup teeters on the edge of a bookcase.

'Just move those paintings off there.'

William points towards a little table covered with papers. I pick up the intricate watercolour paintings; I recognise the indigo blue and rich Venetian red from a set of Winsor & Newton paints I had as a child. An image of my mother sitting on the riverbank, waiting for me to finish yet another painting, flashes through my mind. I rub my fingers gently along the textured paper.

'Did you do these?'

'Mmm.'

'They're beautiful.'

'Thanks. Don't you paint, James?'

'No.'

'Funny, I thought I remembered seeing you painting down by the river. You were much smaller, and your mother used to sit on the bank beside you.'

'I used to paint.'

'Why did you stop?'

I stack the pictures carefully on top of another pile of papers. 'I guess I grew up.'

'Oh, you don't want to do that in a hurry.'

I notice him rubbing his temples, and he notices me watching.

'I've got a tumour growing, James. That's why I'm wobbly.'

'I'm sorry. I don't know what to say.'

'You don't need to say anything. I'm letting you know because I need another favour.'

'What?'

'I need to pay someone to walk with me on the days I can, and to take Juno for walks on the days I can't. I wondered if you'd be interested.'

'Umm. Sorry, I don't think so. I'm not really good with dogs.'

Juno turns around and looks directly at me.

'Well, she seems to think otherwise.'

'I'm not sure how long I'll be around.'

'Are you going somewhere?'

'Yeah, I'm not here for long.' I stand up and take my cup back to the kitchen.

'Well, maybe you could just do tomorrow morning for me. I'll find someone else soon, but it'd really help me.'

'Okay,' I hear myself saying and then start thinking of ways I can get out of it.

'Thanks, James. What time would suit you?'

'Umm, do you have a mobile phone? I could ring in the morning in case something else comes up.'

William winces and closes his eyes as he leans back on the chair.

'Sorry, James. I don't have a mobile phone or a computer. Shall we say nine or ten?'

'Umm. Maybe nine. But if I'm not here, it means something else has come up. I'd better get home.'

'Thanks. I wouldn't ask, but Juno goes crazy without a walk. You'll be extending the lives of lots of plants and shoes.'

All the way home, I wonder how I can get out of it. I mean, it's not my problem that he's dying. It's not my dog.

I just won't turn up.

EMILY

I cross my fingers on both hands as I race along the river walk home, but then remember that two is bad luck and uncross one. *Please let him be held up somewhere.* The curtains are drawn, and a shaft of light at the bottom of the lounge window forewarns me that he's made it home before me. I make my way straight into the kitchen and see the bottle of whisky out on the table. My stomach does a somersault, and I jump when he comes up behind me.

'Where the hell have you been?'

'I had to drop some books off at William's on my way home. I forgot the time.'

'You shouldn't be anywhere near that old fucker. I hear he's got a thing for young girls.'

I want to defend William, but I see the look in Rob's eye and keep my mouth shut tight. I take the leftovers from the fridge.

'Is that it?' he asks.

'What do you mean?'

'No apology. No kiss my arse or nothing.'

'Sorry. I didn't think it would matter.' I move towards the stove, but he grabs my shoulder on the way past.

'Everything matters, Emily. When you've had a hard day, you don't expect to come home to a cold house with no dinner on while your wife is up the road at another man's house.'

'I'm sorry. Your dinner just needs heating.' I go to move, but he pushes my shoulder harder into the wall. I close my eyes, but they spring open when he thrusts his other hand between my legs.

'What were you doing up there, Emily?'

'Nothing, Rob. I was just dropping off some books.'

'Do you like old men, Emily?'

'What?'

'Is that what turns you on, huh?'

'No, he's my friend.'

'I heard he likes watching you.'

'He's lonely. We talk.'

'You talk to him, do you? Does he make you wet?'

'No.' I try to wriggle out of his grip, but he's way too strong, and he pins me to the wall with his body. I smell the alcohol on his breath. He spits some more words at me, but I'm not listening. My mind's racing. He's already past the soothing stage, so I try to work out how to get away. He pauses for a second, and I make a dash for the door, but he throws a leg out and trips me up. My head hits the floor with a thud. I feel his full weight pressing me to the floor. I see the bulge in his pants just as he starts unbuttoning them. I turn my face towards the wall, but he grabs my jaw and pulls it back.

'Look what you make me do.'

'Please, Rob. Don't.'

'Shush.' He puts the palm of his hand over my mouth.

My begging is distorted by his hand, and it sounds like a noise that a wounded animal would make.

I close my eyes and plead with myself to not move. *Do not make a sound. He'll forget you're here, and in a few minutes, it'll be over.*

I get up when he's done and leave him fumbling with his trousers. I edge my way to the bathroom. I lock the door and walk into the shower fully clothed. I turn the tap to hot and wait to feel nothing.

I sleep in my old room, and in the morning, I leave the house without laying out his breakfast things. I let the front door bang behind me.

WILLIAM

I see his uniform through the trees as he comes down the path towards the shed. He's waving a piece of paper in his hand.

'Morning, William,' he says with a smug look on his face. 'I told you I'd be back.' He pokes his head inside the shed. 'Renovations?'

'Huge renovations. I moved a flower vase and changed some cushion covers.'

'I've had a report about some lewd behaviour from you.'

'That's ridiculous.'

'Well, this complaint says otherwise. You were seen taking your clothes off down by the river.'

'This is stupid.' I shake my head and walk back towards the house.

'I wouldn't walk away, William. Do you deny taking your clothes off?'

I stop on the path and stare back at him. 'Some days, if it's hot enough, I jump in the river pool on the way back from my walk. I find it easier to swim without my coat on.'

Juno starts barking, and I turn to see James coming in the gate. He hesitates as he looks at the policeman and then at me.

'Shall I come back?'

Sergeant Norris waves him in. 'Come.'

James walks reluctantly towards us.

'Sergeant Norris. And you are?'

'James.'

'What's your business here, James?'

'Umm.'

'He's my dog walker,' I say to the sergeant and then turn to James. 'Come with me, and I'll get her lead.' As it's clipped on to Juno's collar, she starts tugging James towards the gate.

'Sorry, but would you mind going on your own today?'

'Okay. But where shall I take her?'

'She'll probably drag you across the meadow into the woodlands.'

I watch them with envy as they disappear along the river walkway. The thudding in my temple becomes more insistent, and my tongue searches inside my mouth for saliva. I walk inside to get a drink. The sergeant follows me so closely that

I can feel his breath on my neck. I drink some water and swallow a pill. He takes the pill bottle from me and reads the label.

'"Tramadol. Take two when necessary." What are these for?'

'A headache.'

'Pretty hefty drugs for a headache.'

I walk past him and lie down on the couch. I close my eyes and wait for the painkillers to kick in.

'I'll just have a look around, unless you have any objections.'

'Do what you need to do and go.'

I hear him walking in and out of rooms and opening and shutting cupboards.

'Aha! I think, William, that your problem has just got a whole lot bigger.'

His voice comes from the direction of the kitchen. The pain is still too great for me to open my eyes. I hear his footsteps marching towards me.

'Have you got an explanation for these?'

I open one eye. In one hand, he's holding up a plastic bag of unfilled capsules; in the other, the device I use to suction up the powder.

I close my eye again and shake my head from side to side.

'William. You might want to engage a bit more. I have just found drug-manufacturing equipment, as well as bottles of pills that do not look like they come from a legitimate source.'

'They're not drugs.'

'Then what are they?'

'They're sugar pills.'

'You expect me to believe that you make sugar pills?'

'No. I was just answering your question.'

MARCO

Dad walks into my room in the morning and sits on the end of my single bed.

'How'd it go, Marco?'

'Good. I had heaps of sales.'

'Really?'

'Yeah. Once I moved some of your stuff around, things started selling. You've got too much stock in there, Dad. People can't see anything.'

'Where did you move it to?'

'Out on the pavement.'

'What did you sell?'

'Chairs, tables, lamps.'

'That's great.'

He sits quietly at the end of my bed, and I sense that he's thinking about something other than the shop.

'Are you okay?'

'Yeah. I'm good.'

'I don't think so. What is it? William.'

'Yeah, things didn't go so well yesterday. It's not looking good. They want to see him again tomorrow.'

'He'll be fine.'

'Hope so.'

'He has to be.'

'Yes. For us.' He pushes himself up. 'I made some soup for him. Could you run it over to him when you get up? I'd better get to the shop.'

An hour later, I bang on William's door. Juno gets out of her bed on the porch and sidles over to me.

'William,' I yell and walk in without waiting for him to reply. William's house has been my second home ever since my mother left. After school, he'd always have some fresh juice waiting for me and something sweet to eat in his tins. Even if Dad wasn't working, I'd call in to get my loot.

He comes from the hallway now looking grey and sick, but he attempts a smile when he sees me.

'Sorry, William. Dad wanted me to bring this over.' I hold the pot up in front of me. 'You'll never guess what flavour.'

'Mmm, maybe vegetable?'

'Lucky guess.'

'Come in. Put it in the kitchen and flick the kettle on for me.'

I find a pot under the sink and transfer the soup into it. 'Actually, Dad said it's pea and ham, but think more pea—I didn't see much ham in it.'

'Oh yes. I missed you when it was pea-shelling time. This year it was just me, and he had such a crop. I went to bed that night and dreamt we had to sort them into sizes and count them into bags. I was counting peas for hours.'

'I wouldn't be surprised if that was real life. I'd love to know how many hours we've wasted over the years shelling peas and stacking his stupid pumpkins. We should have sabotaged his vines years ago.'

'Those vines have given us so much. Not just the fruit. You used to love carving pumpkins. I still remember the one featuring an image of me and Juno.'

'I only carved them so Dad would let me have a penknife. What was his rule? You had to know how to use one before you got one.'

I nod. 'You're lucky you got a dad who gave you things to work towards. What about that year that he grew that gigantic pumpkin? People flocked from miles away to have a look.'

'Yeah, the sightseers blocked the traffic on Bridge Street, and Maggie was furious because the locals couldn't get into her shop. That was fun; especially when the pumpkin won big at the autumn festival. We won a hundred pounds.'

'I forgot about the festival. Your dad said you helped with the gala yesterday. How was it?'

'Okay. Same old same old. I think they raised quite a bit of money.'

'Yeah, I heard they were going to use it to make one of those sustainable gardens at the school. I think your dad's going to help. You know, teach kids some life skills.'

'They never bothered to do that stuff when I went to school. It was all "sit down, shut up and read".'

'Every generation thinks they have it harder than the last.'

I put tea leaves in an old Wedgwood pot and take two cups to the table. I have to push plates and a vase of dead flowers out of the way. William has always set up camp around himself. There is usually at least a blanket, a book and a cup. I take a pile of papers from a chair and stack them on the floor. Most of William's beautiful antique furniture is hidden under mounds of clothes, books and old papers.

'So how long are you home for, Marco?'

'Not long, hopefully. I just need to get some money together and get back to the city.'

'What's back in the city? Girlfriend?'

'No.'

'Still chasing the money, eh, Marco? My friend Seneca said, "It is not the man who has too little but the man who craves more that is poor."'

'I would have thought you'd have run out of friends to quote by now. I've been hearing from them for years.'

He smiles and then stumbles backwards. I can see that a bolt of pain has hit him.

'Are you okay?'

'I think so.'

'I'll grab Dad.'

'Don't be silly. I'm fine. Can you pass me that?' He points to a satchel, which rattles as I pick it up. 'Can you get me a drink of water too?'

'I'll get Dad.'

'Marco, I'm not going to die. Well, at least not in this moment. Just stay a little longer. You can distract me with talk until the pain goes away.'

I watch as he eases himself into a chair, then I pass him the water.

'What about that new headmistress at school?' he asks as soon as he's settled.

'That's a strange question, William. Where did that come from?'

'We were talking about girlfriends. Or your lack of one.'

'I'm doing fine. Don't worry about me.'

'I just thought that she seemed nice. Why don't you ask her out?'

'I don't know if she's my type.'

'Oh.' He takes a big sip of water. 'What is your type?'

'I don't think you want to know.'

'I wouldn't ask if I didn't.'

'Okay. I like them easy.'

'Really?'

'Yes. I don't ever intend to keep one.'

'You don't get to keep people, Marco.'

'You know what I mean. It looks like too much hard work.'

'You don't know that.'

'I've got a fair idea. Anyway, where's your wife, then?'

'I left it too late, Marco. All the good ones were gone. There's a lesson in that.'

I shake my head. 'There's always a lesson if you're involved. You missed your vocation. You should have been a schoolteacher, William.'

JAMES

William is sitting on the doorstep when I arrive at nine. He looks pale, but his eyes light up when he sees me.

'I wasn't sure if you'd come back after yesterday. Thanks. Juno, go and get your lead.'

She runs off, and a moment later comes back with the lead in her mouth. She drops it at my feet, and I pat the top of her head as I clip it on her collar. She tugs hard at the lead and nearly pulls me over as she drags me towards the gate. Her tail wags sideways as well as rotating. She barks back at William.

'Alright, I'll come with you this morning.'

The air is warm, but he struggles into a long woollen coat and wraps a scarf around his neck.

'Shall we take the walk along the old railway lines, James?'

'Sure.'

'I love that track. It's like the woodlands on either side of it decided to march down and meet the train. Some fraternising has obviously taken place, as the trees meet at the top, and it's hard now to separate the two counties.'

Juno races off as soon as we reach the woods. William appears to bow to a tree and then waits for me as I hesitate at the entrance. Tall trees with thick canopies stretch as far as I can see. *You can do this,* I tell myself as I step into the woodlands. Every day the simplest of tasks needs more of my effort. Getting up this morning was massive, and several times I doubted that I could do it.

William wanders off the path and weaves his way slowly through the trees. He reaches out and touches some. I've never seen someone in less of a hurry. I'm grateful for the silence and inhale the earthy smell of the forest. William disappears from sight, and after walking on my own for a while, I start to wonder if he's forgotten that he brought me with him. I see him ahead and follow him up a slight incline. He stops under a massive oak tree.

'We should sit here for a moment. It's a good place to watch the show.'

He sits down at the base of the tree and invites me to do the same.

'What show?'

He nods and rests his head on the back of the tree. He pats the ground beside him. 'You'll see.'

I reluctantly sit down. He points to the ground in front of us. 'Look, it started without us.'

Beams of sunlight radiate down through the trees and act like spotlights on the forest floor. The wind makes the leaves above us rustle, and their shadows dance on the ground before us. Tiny butterflies flit between plants, and insects dart along the undergrowth.

William places a finger up to his lips and then smiles at me as he cups his hand around his ear.

At first, all I'm aware of is my thoughts whirling around inside my head, but after a few moments, I notice some space between them. I hear myself sigh and feel a slight breeze. The sound of running water in a nearby stream mixes with the birdsong in the trees. For a moment, I'm aware of something larger than myself. Then the tranquillity is shattered as a small grey squirrel darts out from behind a tree, Juno following closely behind. The chattering inside my head starts up again.

'Well, that was a short show,' William says, pushing himself up. 'Lucky it plays most days.'

We walk in the same direction as Juno. I see her on the path up ahead; she appears to be waiting for us. When we reach her, she races forward a few feet and then stops and starts barking at the base of a conifer tree. I look up and see a squirrel scurrying along a branch. One of my last paintings was of a grey squirrel. I overheard my father telling my mother that she should stop encouraging me to paint: he said my squirrel looked more like a wolf, and painting was for sissies anyway.

We walk back through the woodlands without talking. When we reach William's gate, his skin has a funny tinge of yellow. He ushers me in and then collapses onto a seat made from a tree stump.

'I might have overdone it. I'll be right in a minute. Have a seat.'

I sit down on his overgrown lawn. A shell path winds its way down to a shed draped in ivy.

'What's in the shed?'

'Mainly books. A few people seem to think I might be storing bodies in there. Hmm.'

'Doesn't that bother you? People thinking awful things about you?'

'No. It only matters what I think of myself, and that changes on a daily basis.' William tilts his head skywards and closes his eyes. 'Life's too short to be worried about that sort of stuff, James. Besides, when I don't react to what people are saying, it stops it there. There is no more story.'

'I suppose.'

I hear William inhale sharply. Juno looks up.

'Could you get me a glass of water?'

'Sure.'

As I'm walking across the lawn, he calls out to me.

'There's an envelope on the kitchen bench with some money for the dog walking. It's on top of a white book with silver writing on it. That's for you as well.'

I find both the book and the envelope. I don't count the money, but I see twenty-pound notes in the envelope—it's way too much for walking a dog. I fill a glass with water and take it back to him.

'This is too much.'

'I haven't managed to find anyone else yet. I was hoping you could do the week for me.'

'I'm not sure. I'm still planning on going away.'

'Oh, I understand. I'll sort something. Could we just go with tomorrow?'

I think of Dad and his computer work. 'I'll see. I don't need the book. I have heaps at home I haven't read.'

'You can never have enough books, James. I think of them as medicine. I prescribe at least one dose a day.'

I slide the book into my jacket pocket.

EMILY

The library is the starting point for the walking tour around the village. This morning I offer to escort Fred and Maureen, some tourists, around. Usually, I'd sell them one of the maps that we keep under the counter and point them in the right direction, but this morning I'm keen to get away from Colleen's prying eyes.

I walk slowly, and they potter along beside me as we head towards the old wool store. My thoughts are all over the place.

'Are you alright, dear?' Maureen asks.

'Yes. I'm fine.'

'It's just that you keep sighing.'

'Sorry. I didn't have a good sleep.' I'm keen to move the talk away from me, and point to the excessively large church in the middle of the village. 'The church was completed in 1525. The tower stands at one hundred and forty-one feet.

This makes it the highest village church tower in Britain. It was paid for by Thomas Moir. The locals often refer to it as Thomas Tower. Moir made his fortune by trading the wool that the village was famous for, and he had no family, so he left all his money to the church when he died. His remains are buried in a crypt beneath the church floor. This landmark can be seen from Bellingford, which is over thirty miles away. Do you have any questions?'

Maureen smiles and taps my hand. 'No, you're doing a great job. It's all very interesting, isn't it, Fred?'

'Yes, dear.'

'We've been married over sixty years, you know.'

I fake smile and keep walking.

'How long have you been married?' she asks, nodding towards my wedding band.

'Two. Now, up ahead you'll see the timber-framed guildhall. It's Grade 1 listed and was originally set up as a meeting place for the wealthy wool traders. Over five centuries, it has been used as a prison, a workhouse, an almshouse and even a pub. US troops used it as a social club during the Second World War. It is open every day and run by a group of volunteers.'

Maureen nods her head like she was listening to my spiel but picks up her conversation exactly where she left off.

'My philosophy for a happy marriage is to never go to bed mad. Isn't it, Fred?

'That's right.'

I think of last night and wonder if Maureen would have forgiven Fred if he raped her in the hallway before going to bed.

We have to walk through a narrow lane that goes past the back of the pub. The smell of rotting food coming from the bins makes me retch.

At the guildhall, I push open the wooden doors into a massive entrance hall. On display are stories about the people who once lived here. The wax models are dressed in the woad-dyed woollen cloth that helped make the settlement one of the wealthiest in England in medieval times. Fred ignores the models and makes a beeline to a mummified cat that was found in a chimney cavity.

'Some people believed that it was good luck to bury a cat when you were building,' I tell him. 'Lots of homes built in that time had them.'

I take them upstairs to a room where exhibits of broken toys and bottles of remedies for things like lice and ringworm sit inside glass cabinets.

The ingredients—peacocks' dung, pork lard, crabs' eyes and the dried roots of rare plants—are remnants from the workhouse days.

'When the guildhall was used as a prison, one of the youngest people to be locked up here was an eight-year-old girl.'

'Goodness. What could an eight-year-old have done?' Maureen asks.

'She stole some food and was charged with being an incorrigible rogue. She had no relatives or anybody else to vouch for her, and she was found guilty. They shipped her to Australia.'

'How awful. What happened to her then?'

'No one knows, although there are documents that show that she made it to Australia. I like to think that she found a really nice man and maybe even had some children.'

'Do you have any children?'

'No.'

'We had one, but she died.'

'I'm sorry to hear that.'

'Thanks, but it's just God's way.'

I wonder about 'God's way'. It's hard to believe in a way that takes away children and mothers and leaves behind grandmothers and husbands who hate the sight of you.

'Our daughter was born with lots of challenges, but she made it through to her fifth birthday. We treasure the time we had with her. Isn't that right, Fred?'

'Yes, dear.'

My mind keeps dragging me back to last night. I'm thankful for Maureen's prattle as we wander among the displays. Outside, I show them the walled garden where woad and other plants that they used to dye cloth still grow. She keeps talking even as we climb the steep hill to the church.

'It would have been our daughter's fortieth birthday today, Emily. We light a candle for her every year.'

I show her into the Lady Chapel, where statues of the Virgin Mary and Jesus look down on us.

'Thank you, Emily. This is the perfect place to light one for her.'

She drops a coin into a donation box and takes a small white candle. She lights it from another candle and places it with others on the stand.

I sit in one of the pews as they walk up to the altar. Their backs are towards me, but I watch as they both bow their heads. I presume they're praying. I see him slip his hand into hers, and she turns and smiles at him.

I wanted that. I feel myself getting emotional again. I give myself a moment before calling out to them. 'We'd better keep moving,' I say, herding them out of the church.

On the high street, Maureen stops outside a shop window. She points out a Lilliputian miniature of the church, looking at me and then at Fred.

'Oh. That'll be a nice souvenir of the day. Do you mind, Emily? I collect them.'

'Sure.'

Fred smiles and leans his back against the brick shopfront. 'She loves those funny things.'

Maureen comes out a few minutes later holding a little box. She and Fred beam at each other, and it makes me feel worse. I concentrate on the pain as I bite the insides of my cheeks. The tears are clouding my vision, but I keep my gaze on the ground and stride towards the library.

'We'd better hurry,' I yell back at them.

Flowers are being delivered just as we return. Red roses and purple irises rest on gold paper and cellophane. They're tied up with a massive satin bow and would have cost someone a fortune. I look around at the ladies in the knitting circle, and then the courier driver calls out my name. It takes a moment for me to realise that these flowers are for me. A small envelope is tucked into the cellophane. I open it and read the card inside.

I'm sorry.

'Aren't you just the luckiest girl?' Maureen says as my tears spill over.

Some of the women in the Knit and Natter session ooh and aah, but I notice Maggie looking at me sideways. The problem with being an orphan in a village is that everyone knows your business and thinks they know what's best for you. I'm like the stray cat that everyone feeds—with unwanted advice.

I say a quick goodbye to Maureen and Fred and search for a vase in the kitchen. I find a dusty one under the sink. As I'm arranging the stems in water, Colleen walks up behind me, making me jump.

'God, you scared me.'

She gives me a funny look.

'They're lovely, but you're worth more than a bunch of flowers.'

'I know that.'

'I don't think you do.' She walks away.

Rob surprises me again by meeting me after work. Colleen walks out at the same time I do. The three of us stand awkwardly under the eaves of the porch, and no one says a word. I'm glad that I'm positioned in the middle of them as they glare at each other. Rob insists that we walk along the high street, even though it takes twice as long. I struggle with my bag and the bouquet of flowers. Maggie stops her relentless sweeping outside the post office long enough to stare at us as we walk by.

'Can I help you with anything, Maggie?' Rob calls across the street.

I tug on his arm to keep walking.

'You don't fool me,' she calls down the street after us.

I feel the muscles in Rob's arm tense, and I notice my body does the same. He looks down at me, and for a moment I think he's angry, but then his face softens.

'I'm sorry, Emily. People like her get to me; sticking their noses into other people's lives. I let things get to me when I know I shouldn't.'

'You hurt me, Rob.'

'It's like something takes over, and it's not really me.'

'But it was you.'

'I know.'

'It was horrible, and you scared me.'

He stops walking and stares at me.

'It won't happen again.'

I search his eyes. Looking for some sign that he means it.

'Give me another chance, Emily. It won't happen again. I promise.'

We walk past the newsagent. On the cover of the newspaper is a photo of hundreds of tourists on a beach in Europe. They've flocked there trying to cool off in a freak heatwave. All of a sudden, I know what we need.

'We should go on a holiday, Rob.'

'Mmm.'

'It could be like our belated honeymoon. You always said we were going to go later.'

'Did I?'

'We could both do with a holiday. Get away from here. It'll be like a new start.'

He frowns, but then he smiles and nods his head.

'You should look into it.'

'I'd love to do that.' My face feels like it might crack open if I smile any harder. I'm finally getting to leave the village—and, even better, I'm going with my husband. As we're walking, I start fantasising about all the places we could go. I don't know why I didn't think of this before.

In the morning, for the first time ever, I don't want to go to work, but then I remember that the preschool kids from the neighbouring village are coming today.

Colleen starts as soon as I arrive.

'A bunch of flowers and all is forgiven.'

'You don't know what you're talking about.' She follows me as I move to the back of the library. 'It was you who told me to always look for the good in someone. Why can't you be happy for me?'

'What do you want me to say, Emily? That I think Rob's a great bloke?'

'You just don't know him.'

'I know his type, Emily. That's enough for me. You're still holding on to the fairy tale. It's your business, and I'm trying to stay out of it, but I'm just letting you know that I don't like what I see.'

'Well, you're right about one thing.'

'What?'

'It's my business. And by the way, I'll need to book some leave. Rob and I are going on holiday.'

WILLIAM

Juno's barking in the garden wakes me up from my slumber on the window seat. I look out the window and see Sergeant Norris talking to James by the gate. Juno is tapping at the gate with a paw and looks like she's about to leap over. The sergeant hands James a card and leaves.

I push myself up and wipe my eyes and slap my cheeks as Juno rushes in.

'Come in, James. I'm in the lounge.' I force a smile onto my face when I see him.

'Did she behave?'

'Not really.' James pats her head, and I'm glad to see a faint smile at the corner of his mouth.

'I hope Sergeant Norris didn't give you too much of a hard time. He's just marking his new territory.'

'He wanted to know if you'd ever offered me drugs.'

We both look towards the kitchen. I know he would have seen the stuff on the bench.

'Mmm, the sergeant seems to have added two and two together and come up with six. He thinks I'm manufacturing drugs. He took away some pills. When he analyses them, he'll find out that it's just sugar.'

'You sell sugar pills?'

'No. I give them away.'

'Why do you have sugar pills?'

'It's a long story, James, but basically I give them to people when I think they need something to believe in.'

'Is that what you do in your shed? Give people pills?'

'Very rarely.'

'What do you do, then?'

'Usually ... I just listen. People want to tell their stories. People need to be heard. And sometimes I lend them a book.'

'I still don't understand why you give them the pills.'

'Same reason I give them a book. There's hope in them. There's a belief that all will be well. We need to know that.'

MARCO

I drag the ladder through the hole in the hedge and lean it against William's house. Some plonker has tagged the front of his house in red paint again.

I soak a rag in petrol and climb up the ladder. Ever since I was a boy, there has always been someone throwing something at William's house: rotten fruit, eggs. It seems to be a crime in this village to be different, or even to try to keep to yourself. William just sprays off the offending garbage and never says a word about it.

I look down now and see him coming from the side of his house.

'Ah. My fairy godmother,' he says, looking up at me.

'Whatever, William.' The paint comes off easily, but it leaves an imprint of the word NUTTER on the house. I climb down the ladder.

'I don't know how you stay in this hole.'

'It's easy. It's a nice hole.'

'What's nice about it?'

'Lots. The woodlands, the river and the people.'

'Including the person who did this?'

He shrugs his shoulders. 'There's no point in being angry.'

'Yeah, there is. Whoever did this is an arsehole, William. You need to track them down and deal with them.'

'Haven't you heard that saying, Marco? Holding on to anger is like drinking poison and expecting the other person to die. It's probably a bunch of kids. I'm the witch in the village who you throw stuff at. I'm okay with that.'

'I don't get it. Maybe they're right, William. Maybe you are a nutter.'

He laughs. 'All I'm saying is that most of the time, it's easier to let go than hold tight.'

'Whatever you say, William.'

'I say come inside and get some jars of relish.'

I follow him inside. A tea chest is in the middle of his lounge, and cardboard boxes are scattered all over the floor.

'Planning on going somewhere?'

'I thought I was.'

I remember about the tumour and quickly change the subject.

'Where's that relish?'

He smiles and then stumbles a little. He leans on the back of a chair to steady himself and then carries on like nothing happened.

'It's on the bench.'

'I'd better get these to Dad. I'll come back for the ladder later.'

'Don't run away, Marco. You don't need to be frightened by my illness.'

'How can you be so accepting, William? This could kill you.'

'Maybe, but we all have to die at some stage. It's about the only thing we can be sure of.'

'It's just wrong.'

'It just is, Marco. One thing I've grasped in my lifetime is that life flows much better when I accept what's happening. I've tried fighting against it, and lost every time.'

I shake my head. 'They're right. You're a nutter.'

JAMES

Juno races along the track in front of me. I call out her name, but she doesn't return. I listen for sounds of her but hear nothing except the chirping of the thrushes in the trees. Up ahead the path splits into three. I stand at the junction and listen. The ground is carpeted in the gold and scarlet of autumn leaves. The colours play tricks with my eyes and give off an almost magical light. An argus butterfly drifts down and settles on a bush beside me. The different shades of brown remind me of the mallard ducks down by the river. I call again, and this time I hear a bark in the distance. I clamber up the bank towards the sound and into a wooded section off the path. I follow a line of trees, keeping the church tower as a landmark on my right.

Nature whispers to all my senses, and a feeling of warmth floods through my body. It's fleeting, but the trees and the wildlife have let me sense something other than the relentless voice inside my head. It makes me feel connected. It's the same feeling I got when I painted. I could leave everything at the top of the bank and slide down into a different world. All that mattered was being beside the river, with the wildlife, and the brush strokes on the paper. I remember being happy.

I wander through a small stream at the bottom of the path, and my thoughts continue to tumble. The thought that I was once happy seems as crazy as coming across a twin I didn't know I had. Juno's bum and her wagging tail appear on one side of a bush; the rest of her is hidden. 'There you are.' She pops her head up and comes running back to me. She nuzzles her nose into my hand. 'What are you up to?' I barely have time to scratch under her mouth before she takes off again.

I follow the stream and sit down beside it for a moment. Juno fossicks around in the fallen leaves. I listen to the trickle of water as it meanders its way across some of the pebbles. The stillness envelopes me.

If I was once happy, maybe I could be again?

EMILY

I find Colleen in the small bedroom off the kitchen. The wooden doors are open, and she sits on the steps that lead out to the garden. Her shoulders move with the sound of her sobbing. I take a few steps back but knock into a stool and send it crashing to the ground. Colleen swipes at her face and then picks up a book from the stack next to her. She stays facing out towards the garden.

'I've been meaning to get onto these for a long time.'

'I'll go and make us our tea.'

I spoon tea leaves into the big pot and let it brew for a long time. Colleen has composed herself completely when I return with the tea. I take a seat on a wooden chest at the base of the bed.

'I think we have to face up to the fact, Emily, that we are going to be forced to move.'

'There must be something we can do? Can't we protest?'

'I don't think it will help. The church has to sell the manse to finance the footings of the church. If they don't redo the footings, then they'll lose the church as well.'

'We can't lose the manse. Couldn't we do some fundraising? Do some cake stalls and sell some things?'

'That's a great idea, but we would need thousands of pounds.'

'We can't let them move us.'

'I don't think we have a say in it.'

'But where will we go?'

'They were thinking of putting us in the old annexe by the community hall.'

'That's a horrible building. It's ugly and it's cold. We wouldn't even fit the books in there. People will have to take turns at coming in.'

'There's been talk that our library could merge with Bellingford's one. They already have a purpose-built library building.'

'But how will we get to Bellingford every day?' I see the look on Colleen's face, and I know that there will be no commuting to Bellingford. 'Oh. I'm so slow. When we lose the library, I lose my job. That's right, isn't it?'

I see the tears pool in her eyes as she nods her head.

WILLIAM

I edge my way down the bank and slide into the river where the reeds are not so thick. The river has only just taken off her night clothes, and the water is icy cold. It sends a shock through my body and makes me gasp. I let the current take me away from the land and feel like I've stepped outside of time as I float downstream towards the bridge. Nature invites me in and makes me feel like I'm a part of it. I feel myself getting cold and breaststroke towards the bank. I clamber out over slippery river rocks covered in emerald green moss. I startle some nesting birds as I race along the walkway to collect my clothes. I watch the birds take off and feel the same soaring in my own body.

MARCO

I look at my phone and see that I've missed three calls from Owen, but he hasn't left a message. I slide the phone back into my pocket. He can wait. I knew he'd regret his decision. It's going to feel so nice to make him grovel.

Dad walks in from the garden with bits of straw attached to his overalls.

I watch as he struggles to get his legs out of his clothing, and I realise that he's getting older.

'Can I make you a cuppa, Dad?'

'What? What have you done with my Marco? He doesn't offer to make tea.'

'Haha. I was just going to make one, and you look like you could do with one.'

He slumps down into a chair. 'That would be really nice. I'm knackered. I swear those pumpkins get heavier each year I stack them.'

'Yeah, I'm sure it's the pumpkins.'

He smiles but ignores my dig. 'Did you see William this morning?'

'Briefly, but I'll pop over again later.' My phone rings, and I see that it's Owen again. 'I'd better take this, Dad.'

He pushes himself up from his chair. 'I'll make us the tea, eh?'

I nod as I move down the hall. I try to act nonchalant on the phone, but the truth is that I'll take anything Owen's offering. I can hear in Owen's voice how hard it is for him to need something from me. I play with him as long as I can.

'That was my old boss, Dad.'

'Did you get your job back?'

'Nearly. He wants me to source something for him. I'll need to make up some flyers and get them printed. Does the post office still do that shit?'

Dad shakes his head as I move past him.

'Yes, Marco. They still print things. Your tea's on the bench.'

'If my flyer doesn't attract ducks to the pond, nothing will.'

'Now, that nonsense sounds more like my Marco.'

I spend the afternoon making up a flyer to put in a few letterboxes.

'I'm just going into town,' I yell out to Dad in the garden. 'I'll see if William needs anything.' A gloved hand waves out from the side of the shed.

On the path to William's door, small branches poke out from the hedge; I snap one off as I pass. William would never let the hedge get this long unless he was really sick. Telling him that I'm going to cut it should be the fastest way to get him back on his feet.

'Hey, William. I'm going in to the post office, and I wondered if you needed anything.'

'Thanks, Marco, but I can't think of anything. I need your help with something else though.'

'What's that?'

'I was wondering if you'd be interested in selling some of my antiques. I'll pay you a commission.'

'I don't know much about antiques—except that yours are worth a fortune.'

'But you know about selling. I know the history behind them. Most of them were my grandmother's— she inherited them from her mother.'

'Some of them look really valuable. You should get someone who deals in antiques to come and assess them. There's bound to be someone you can find on the internet.'

'I don't know about all that stuff, and I'm not keen on having strangers in my home. I'd rather have you do it.'

'Okay, I'll look into it. I better go get this stuff printed.'

'Thanks, Marco.'

I wander down to the post office and have to pay Reg a ridiculous sum of money to print my flyer and to put it into some of the boxes. No wonder he owns so much property in the area. All I need is for one person to take the bait, and my commission cheque will set me up in a new place far away from here.

JAMES

That evening Mum piles my plate with mashed potatoes, cauliflower and corned beef.

'I can't eat this, Mum.'

'What do you mean, you can't eat this?' Dad says, staring at me and holding his knife and fork up like soldiers beside his plate. 'I've had enough of this. What did you say you've been doing with your days?'

'I didn't.'

'And why is that?'

I shrug my shoulders, but he continues to stare.

'No one asked me.'

'Do you know who he's been seen with?' he says, glaring at my mother.

She shakes her head. 'Does it matter?'

'Of course it bloody matters. It's that lunatic up the road. The guy who hugs trees and jumps in the river. I introduced myself to the new policeman—and you can imagine my surprise when he said he'd met my son up at William's house. The whole town's probably talking about it.'

I let out a sigh and go to get up from the table.

'I'm just walking his dog.' This conversation and the effort of stringing so many words together exhaust me. 'If you don't mind, I need to lie down.'

'I do mind. You'll stay here until I've finished. Have you been in his house?'

I look down at the table.

'I'll take that as a yes.'

He pushes himself up from the table.

'Jesus, James. What the hell were you doing in there?'

'Nothing.'

'Nothing. You went to a known deviant's house and did nothing.'

'He's not a deviant.'

'Oh. You know him well, do you?'

'That's enough, Raymond!'

'I'm just asking a simple question. How well?'

I concentrate on a tiny grain of sugar.

'You know what people say about him, James? What do you think they'll be saying about you?'

I have to get out of the room. He yells at the back of me as I leave.

'I forbid you to go back to his house.'

EMILY

I read the instructions again, in case I'm reading them wrong. I hold the strip at the coloured end, like it tells me to, and dip the end with the arrows into a cup of my urine. I lie the stick flat down and start timing for ten minutes. I look at it sideways after only five minutes, and just like on the sample before, I see the two pink lines appearing. I sit down on the side of the bath and place the stick in my pocket.

I get a sick feeling in the pit of my stomach when I think about telling Rob, but a bigger part of me feels excited. I'm going to be a mother. Rob's made it pretty clear that he doesn't like children—but maybe he'll change his mind if it's one of his own.

Just when I thought nothing could ever be right again, I get a miracle. Even the thought of losing the manse now doesn't feel like the end of the world. This baby is the beginning of my world.

I lay strips of baking paper inside the muffin tins and roll out the pastry, then line the tins. I tip breadcrumbs into a mixing bowl and squeeze in the sausage meat, along with the bacon, sage and mace. I grind in salt and pepper, and wonder if I'll get a boy or a girl. I squish the mixture in my hands, divide it and spoon it into the tins. I won't mind either way what sex the baby is. I just know I'll love it. I stamp out circles from the remaining pastry and brush egg over the tops. No wonder I've felt so rotten. As I press the pastry edges together, I wonder what Colleen will think. She'll probably feel awful about all her meanness. I hear Rob's keys in the door and quickly wipe my hands on my apron.

'I'm making pork pies for dinner,' I call out. 'Mini ones so you'll have some for work.'

He walks straight into the lounge.

I sprinkle sesame seeds on the top of the pies and put them in the oven. I wipe out his tumbler and pour in a double measure of whisky. I take him the tumbler. I judge by the creases in his brow that I need to give him a bit more time before breaking the news.

I sit on a bar stool for twenty minutes and watch the pies turn brown. I wait until they're a perfect golden colour before pulling them out.

I open the hall door so the smell will snake its way to the lounge.

I wait until he's eaten one of the pies and is tucking into the second one.

'Rob. I have something to tell you.'

'What.'

'We're having a baby.'

His head whips away from the television.

'We're what?'

'I'm pregnant.'

'No, you're not.'

'I checked three times.'

'You're not having a baby.' He turns back to the television and pushes the volume up on the remote.

'But ... I want to,' I say loudly.

He pushes the volume button again and shakes his head.

'You can't even look after us properly.'

I feel the blood rush to my face. I pick up his lunchbox from the floor and take it into the kitchen. I open the lid and see that the lunch I made him hasn't been touched. My hands are shaking. And then something inside me snaps. All the tension of the last few weeks races through my body. I march back into the lounge.

'Rob, I want to have this baby.'

'I can't hear you.'

I grab the remote and push mute. He glares at me.

'What's got into you? Give me that remote.'

I put it behind my back.

For a while, he doesn't answer, but then his jaw juts out and his lips spread tight across his teeth.

'I'll give you three seconds to give it back.'

WILLIAM

Juno pulling on the end of my sleeve wakes me up. I squint hard and press the palm of my hand against my temple. When I try opening my eyes, one of them takes a lot longer. I'm starting to see signs daily of parts of my body not responding to messages. I feel a sloppy lick on my face.

'Okay, thanks, Juno. I'm awake.'

I push the blanket off and myself up from the couch. I open the windows and sip in a big breath of air. It's getting harder each morning to get moving, but I'm so grateful to be given another day. I gulp down some water and take two pills from my pocket.

Juno bounds across the lawn to James with the lead in her mouth. Judging by his body language, he looks as bad as I feel.

'Morning, James.'

'Hi.' He sits down on the porch step, and Juno comes and licks his hand.

'Not today, Juno.'

'Are you alright, James?'

'No. I'm sorry, William, but I can't do this any more.' He scratches under Juno's chin. 'I'm going away in the next few days.'

A vision of him under the bridge pops into my head. I ease myself down onto the step next to him and feel constriction around my heart. I leave a gap between us and nod my head but don't say anything. I hope that he might carry on talking, but he doesn't.

'James. I have to tell you something about myself.'

He doesn't look up but continues staring at his feet.

'When I was your age, I went to study medicine. A career that I should never have chosen—for lots of reasons, but I chose it because I knew it would make my father happy. I wanted him to be proud of me, I wanted to please him. I spent seven years studying for someone else's dream.'

I look across. Although he hasn't moved, I can see that he's listening to me.

'I worked long hours in cold, dark hospitals and hardly ever saw the sun. I hated my job, but I had no idea how to change it. The longer I was a doctor, the more disillusioned I became. I was convinced that one of the biggest influences on a patient's health and recovery wasn't what we prescribed them, but their belief in their own wellbeing. I did my own sugar pill trials and felt like I was getting close to some truth. I was starting to see some positive signs that my theory was right.'

He looks up at me for a moment, but then he drops his head again.

'The hospital found out what I was doing, and I was struck off and narrowly avoided jail. My father never spoke to me again, but I did receive a letter from him, telling me that he no longer had a son and would prefer it if I did not use his family name. I'd worked out by then that I was never going to please him anyway. I actually felt a sense of relief when I gave myself a new name.'

James draws lines on the dirt with his feet.

'Why are you telling me all of this?'

'I'm making the point that, in letting go of the person I thought I should be, I stumbled on a more truthful version of me. Someone I could live with. I kept thinking I needed to be a better me, but I just needed to be. I believe you're struggling with the same things, James.'

He doesn't say anything, but I see the tears pool in his eyes. I want to reach out to him, but I keep the space between us. The pain inside my head feels like something is about to explode. I close my eyes to get away from the light. The thumping is constant. He swipes away a tear, and I feel a heaviness in the pit of my stomach as he goes to leave. I will myself to stay seated as he pushes himself to stand. I want to hold on to him and beg him to stay. I keep swallowing, hoping to find more saliva, but there is nothing in my mouth. I need water, but I feel like I might fall if I stand. He slowly walks away. When he's gone from sight, I crawl back inside. Juno stays by my side and licks my face when I stop for a rest. I spend the rest of the day slipping in and out of sleep when the painkillers offer me respite.

MARCO

I meet the restaurateur and his accountant outside the building at 2p.m. The restaurateur is feigning disinterest and lets his accountant do all the talking. I can see from his eyes, though, that he's taken with the beautiful Tudor building before we've even entered it. I took a gamble on placing a few costly advertisements in a London paper; within twenty-four hours, I've reeled in my first bite.

'There's a few people involved with the sale of the building, and it's a bit contentious at the moment, so I need you to be discreet.' I push open the oak doors into the library. I'm grateful to see that it's empty except for the forlorn-looking girl behind the counter. I've seen her around the village, but I have no idea what her name is. I'm relieved when I spot her name badge.

'Morning, Emily. These gentlemen are thinking of moving to our village, so I'm just showing them around.'

She nods but doesn't really look at us, and disappears behind a bookshelf. Upstairs I get a chance to tell them about the timber that was cut from the surrounding woodlands and point out the pressed ceiling and ornate fireplace surrounds. The man is trying hard not to smile as he listens to the history of the building. He's already planning his new restaurant.

'This space would make a great meeting room, or a place to hold small functions. There are separate toilets on this level, and there is already a dumb waiter that connects to the downstairs kitchen. This area, with its wonky buildings, has become quite the little hotspot. Just last week, it was featured in *The Guardian* as one of the best villages close to London for a weekend away.'

We get to the Swan at three, and I'm glad to see that the place is pretty much empty. I take them to a booth at the back by the stone fireplace and away from prying eyes. I place some paperwork on the table, and we get straight down to business.

'How long is it going to be before the existing tenants can move out?' he asks me.

'The church owns the building, along with a lot of the other buildings in the village. The council pays them a fee to house the library. Three of the five committee members have agreed that they should sell the manse, but on the proviso that the library is given the time it needs to find new premises and relocate.

His brow creases. 'So, what time frame am I looking at?'

'Maybe a month—at worst maybe two.'

'Well, why don't you come back to me when you have an empty building to sell. If I haven't found something else by then, perhaps I'll still be interested.'

'The property isn't on the market as yet, but I can assure you that the moment it goes on, there will be a lot of interest. I think if we placed an offer on the table now, it might help the committee speed up their thinking and keep you ahead of the pack. Let me know, and I can draw up a contract.'

JAMES

At the end of the riverside path, I step over the trunk of a fallen elder and into the meadowland that borders the river. The cold, murky waters soak into my trousers and come halfway up my shins. I use the bank to support me as I wade downstream. The increasing current forces me to climb back up the bank. I know this corner well; I nearly drowned in it as a child. There's a hidden hole where the depth of the water changes from knee high to over your head in an instant. The only thing that saved me was the roots of an elder that had fingered out over the water and then tucked back in on themselves. I clung to them and was wondering how much longer I could hold on when a man punting down the river saw me and rescued me. I was wrapped in river weed and stank of mud as he pulled me onto his punt. The local newspaper ran a story about my rescue and the dangers of young people playing by the river.

Walking in the woodlands with Juno and William reminded me of my childhood refuge. The place I came to every chance I got, until my near drowning got me banned from going near the river on my own.

I wander along the narrow path, hoping that some part of the ruin survived. I slide back down the bank when I see the edges of the bricks. I pull back some fallen branches and bracken. Some of the bricks have crumbled a little, but the main structure of the Second World War pillbox still stands strong. I instinctively walk around to the left and guide myself along the wall. I crawl into the space at the back of the ruins and use my hands to pull myself through the tunnel made by fallen bricks and trees. It opens up into a bigger area, but it's still cloaked in darkness. I take a few more tentative steps along the wall. I used to come here and dream about how great life was going to be when I grew up. I wish I could go back and tell that boy to enjoy the moment. Some of those days turned out to be the best.

In the corner of the structure, I feel around until I touch the edges of a wooden box. I've gouged my name along the top of it. *James Farndale. Famus artest.* The catch is stiff and comes off in my hands as I open it. Inside is my metal paint tin. The paints inside are rock hard; nearly all are empty. I see my small fingerprints on the tubes where I pressed down hard to get a little more paint out. No amount of squeezing will bring these paints to life now. My sketch pad has been nibbled by vermin, but evidence of my secret paintings is scattered at the bottom of the box. I pick up a handful of the colourful scraps and let them fall like confetti.

I walk to the spot where a shaft of light shines down and illuminates the dirt floor. I know it like an old friend, and the earthy smell comforts me as I lie down in this space. The only sound I hear is my breathing. In this stillness, it feels like everything drops away, just like it does in the woodlands. I cup my hands behind my head and look up into the sky. I used to believe that I'd found the portal to another world here; all I had to do was find a way to climb up the light. There is only my breath and the vivid blue sky above.

I hear the voice inside my head start chattering, but I feel a distance from it. There is a me that is lying on the ground observing the thoughts like an outsider. I watch and listen as a new thought comes in. For a second, the world freeze-frames. *Are there two of me?* I'm so shocked by this thought that for a moment I can't move. I feel a separateness from my thoughts. *Is it possible that the voice inside my head is not real?*

EMILY

There's a moment when my eyes open, and before the light seeps in, that I feel whole. My hands reach for my stomach and then I feel a chill as I remember where I am.

He told the nurse that I'd fallen down the stairs, but I don't think she believed him. I said it was the truth when she asked me the first time, and I lied again when she repeated her question when Rob was out of the room. All I wanted was for them to stop asking questions and save my baby. They said it was nature's way when they couldn't, which makes no sense at all. I'd already hugged that baby in my arms. Watched her smile and breathed in her scent.

Every time I wake up, Rob is sitting beside my bed. He's hardly left my side and just keeps saying over and over how sorry he is. How things got on top of him again, and he didn't mean to. He said he'll get some help. He said that, as soon as I get out, we're going to book our tickets for our holiday. He brought in some maps of Scotland, and has stuck them on the wall where I can see them each time I open my eyes.

I want to believe him so badly.

He goes to get himself a coffee, and a moment later William arrives, looking like one of the patients. His face is a pale shade of grey, and he's leaning heavily on a walking stick. He sinks down onto a chair next to the bed, and I can hear his laboured breath.

'Are you alright, William?'

'Yes. You don't look very good though.'

'I'm okay.'

He nods and looks at my swollen face before quickly turning away.

'Emily, I don't have much time left. We need to talk about something.'

I blush, and this time the heat flushes through my whole body.

'Does everyone know?'

'What?'

'Is everyone talking about me and Rob?'

'I don't know, but I wouldn't worry about what other people are thinking. You need to think about what you want to do from here.'

I don't realise I'm crying until William brushes a tear from my cheek.

'I'm so ashamed.'

'You have nothing to be ashamed of, Emily. You did nothing wrong.'

'I don't know what to say.'

'You don't have to say anything. But you could let people help you. A lot of people care about you. I know my timing is off, but I have to tell you something before I run out of time. Something that I should have told you years ago.'

'What?'

'I knew your mother.'

'How would you know my mother, William?'

'I met her at Waverly.'

'You were at Waverly? The mental hospital.'

'Briefly.'

'You were a patient?'

'Yes. I lost myself for a while. I met your mother just after you'd been taken from her.'

'It can't have been her, William. My mother gave birth to me and then ran away. She killed herself not long after.'

'She didn't run away. She was fifteen and struggling with her mental health. She said that everyone agreed except her that her baby would be better off in the care of her mother.'

'Are you sure? My mother's name was Mary Ocket.'

'I'm sure.'

'I was taken from her?'

'Yes. She took that as proof that she was unworthy to be a mum. I told her that the fact that she'd memorised every little detail about you, in such a small time, showed me that she would make a great mum. We walked around the gardens and down to the pond most days. She talked about Radley: the woods and the river. But she mainly talked about you, and how perfect you were.'

'She said that I was perfect?'

'She did.'

'Then how could she leave me?'

'She wasn't thinking straight. Her thoughts would have been telling her things that just weren't true. She convinced herself that anybody would do a better job than she could.'

'Mothers aren't supposed to kill themselves.'

'No. They're not. Lots of things aren't supposed to happen, Emily, but they do. This is the hardest part of what I have to tell you.'

There is a strange feeling in my body. A shiver that creeps up my back.

'They gave your mother some pills. I think that's what killed her.'

I lean back on the pillow. I can feel my brow crease.

'She didn't overdose. She drowned herself.'

'Yes, but I believe that the drug they prescribed for her became toxic in her system and gave her those suicidal thoughts. I looked it up when I eventually got well, and those drugs should never have been given to a fifteen-year-old. She was depressed and grieving. She needed someone to talk to, and we failed her.'

'You can't be to blame for that, William.'

'I felt her restlessness, and her need to keep moving, in my own body as soon as she started taking the pills. I have a thing called mirror-touch synaesthesia. In part, this means that I experience a sensation that another person feels in my own body. I could feel her spinning like she was on a carousel. I didn't want the doctors to think I was going even crazier, so I said nothing. She drowned herself in the pond a few weeks after beginning to take those pills.'

'Wow.' I shake my head as I try and imagine what that must feel like. Some days my own feelings are too much. No wonder he keeps mainly to himself. A sharp pulling in my lower abdomen reminds me of another loss. I breathe deeply until the pain subsides. I take a sip from my water and offer some to William. He looks like he might be in more trouble than me.

'My mother made the choice. Not you, William. Why didn't you tell me you knew her though?'

'You were just a little girl when I came to the village. I wasn't even sure I'd find you.'

'You came here to find me?'

'Yes, but my reasons were selfish. I thought if I could see that you were okay, then maybe I could be too. I should have told you, but it never seemed to be the right time. I wanted to apologise too, but I could never find the words. When I sensed that you were struggling, I figured the least I could do was stay and keep an eye on you.'

'What did my mother look like?'

'Exactly like you.'

'I look like my mother. Huh … I've always wanted to know what she looked like. My grandmother didn't keep any photographs of her. No wonder she hated me; I must have been a constant reminder.'

A nurse comes in and seems shocked to see me sitting up.

'I thought you'd still be out. How's the pain?'

'It hurts.'

'What does?'

'Everything.'

WILLIAM

I feel a pressure under my ribs and a ripping in my lower abdomen as I sit with Emily. My bottom lip feels tight and sore when I look at hers. I concentrate on the sterile equipment around me to distract myself from her pain. The nurse gives her some medication, and her breathing becomes softer.

'When you were lost, William—how did you find yourself again?'

'It was gradual. I think I slowly accepted myself with all my flaws. After your mother died, my shame and sorrow plunged me into a darkness so black it felt impossible to believe in any light. I was incapable of doing anything, but I read. Little by little, those stories helped me find my way out.'

'What stories?'

'No specific one. I read everything. Initially, most of the tales were dark and intense; those were the ones that spoke to me most. After a while, I gravitated towards the stories about hope and redemption. Your mother spoke about walking in the woodlands that surround Radley and swimming in the waterholes in summer. That was the place she felt most at peace. I started reading a lot of books about the healing powers of nature. Eventually, I ended up here, and I walked in her woods and swam in her river. Over time I felt better.'

'I'd like to do that. Go walking in the woods.'

'It's a magical thing to do. Nature takes our breath away and breathes new life into us.'

She tries to smile, but her swollen lip stops it halfway. She sags back onto the pillows behind her.

'I'll leave you to rest.'

Her colours are fragmented, and she feels as fragile as spun toffee, yet her core remains untouched and golden.

MARCO

Beatrice squealed in my ear when I told her what she might be offered for the manse. A lot of the people living here would have no idea that their houses are worth a fortune. Old Mr Anderson, for example: never once left the village. When he died, they carried him up the high street in a pine coffin and into the cemetery only a mile from the house he'd been born in. His house sold for well over a million pounds, and yet he had lived like a pauper.

I'd forgotten how much I love chasing a sale. The thought of it has me reminiscing about my first few years in London, when people were basically begging me to sign them up. The difference between me and the other agents was that I paid attention. I could spot an ego that needed to be stroked, and I learnt the fine art of cajoling the not-so-brave. I love the thrill of sealing the deal, but I get just as much fun from the games beforehand. I know that

Beatrice would like nothing better than a speedy sale so she can get the repairs under way before Christmas. She'll get all the kudos for being the one to save St Peter's. My tease that she might just get a plaque in the church for her forethought met with another squeal. I know that the restaurateur has a big ego. I haven't quite worked out how to play this yet, but I know I will. I made another call to him to assure him that things were moving forward nicely and reiterated that such a magnificent property was worth being patient for.

I'm excited, and I feel like celebrating, but it's not much fun celebrating on your own. I grab two bottles of beer from the fridge and find Dad around the back of the shed. I pass him one of the bottles.

'Here's to not having to put up with me much longer, Dad.' I chink my bottle against his and take a swig, but I notice that he just holds on to his.

'I don't really want to drink to that, Marco. I like having you here. This is your home.'

'Thanks, Dad, but I need to keep moving. You know, make something of myself.'

He puts the beer on the bench and stares at me. 'Marco, I've never understood what it is you think you need to make yourself into. To me, you are already something.' He picks up the rake, wanders down to the back lawn and starts pulling the leaves into piles.

'The wind is just going to come and blow them all away again,' I yell out to him. He shrugs his shoulders and carries on raking.

JAMES

I pick up the books from my bedside table and squash them into my chest. I put them in the front pocket of my backpack and walk fast along the river walk. I wanted to say goodbye to my parents, but I wasn't brave enough. I knock on William's door, but no one answers. I place the books on the armchair on the porch. I start to walk away, but Juno's bark stops me. She scratches on the inside of the door and leaps out to greet me when I open it.

When I enter the house, I hear a small noise. Further in, I find William crumpled up on a bed in the lounge.

'William?' I walk over to him, and he opens his eyes. He attempts a smile, but his mouth hardly moves, and he has no real colour to his face. A small bit of spit dribbles from the side of his mouth.

'I was hoping you'd come back.' He slurs his words.

I wipe the dribble off his chin with my shirt. 'Are you okay?'

He attempts a smile. 'Probably not.'

'I'll go get some help.'

'No, don't. I'm okay. Arlo's just gone next door to get me something. He'll be back in a minute. How are you?'

'Alright. I just came to say goodbye.'

'What?' He winces and tries to push himself up.

'I'm leaving on this morning's train.'

'Oh.'

'I need to get away and work some things out for myself. Remember when you said that all I needed to be was me? I realised that I don't know who that is—I've spent years trying not to be me. I need to look at that, and I don't think I can do that here.'

He nods his head but says nothing.

'I feel like the woods helped plug me back in, and the books helped me find my way home. I know I have a long way to go, but at least I have some hope, and I can see a future.'

I stack the books beside his bed. 'Thank you, William, for everything.'

'I didn't do anything,' he croaks.

'You listened.'

I look at my watch and see that I have to make my way to the station. I walk fast and hear the train in the distance. I purchase a ticket and sit on a bench outside. Juno races along the platform as a whistle screeches, and I see the train coming down the track. I give her a pat and take the bag that's tied around her neck. A few people get off the train, and the conductor looks along the platform and signals for me to get on. I push Juno away. 'Go on home now, girl.' She licks my hand and sprints from the station. I take a seat in the last carriage and see Juno sitting in the middle of the overbridge. I stare out the train window until Juno and Radley disappear. I open the bag and pull out a metal paint set. A note is taped to the front of it. William's writing is nearly illegible, but he's pressed so hard that I can trace the letters with my finger.

'"To thine own self be true"—Shakespeare.'

EMILY

'We need to run a few more tests on you, Emily,' the nurse says and then turns towards Rob. 'It's going to take a few hours, so I suggest you have a break, Mr Merton.'

'I'll stay.'

'I'm sorry, but I need to insist. We'll be as quick as we can, but we need at least an hour.'

Rob juts his jaw out, and I see his clenched teeth, which is a sign that he's about to explode.

'You can wait downstairs in the cafeteria if you don't feel like going out, but Emily's needs come first.'

Rob glares at the nurse, but she stares straight back at him.

'I can get security to fetch you when we're done.'

'I don't need anyone fetching me. I'll be back in an hour.' He storms out of the room.

'What tests are you going to do?'

'I'm just going to take a few blood samples. It won't take long.'

Colleen pokes her head around the door a few minutes later. I expect the nurse to throw her out, but she finishes taking my blood and smiles at us both.

'Don't be too long. She needs all the rest she can get.'

Colleen wraps her arms around me. I inhale her scent of rose water—it comforts me but also makes me want to cry. I stay in her embrace as long as I can. I see her looking at the bruises on my arms. I am relieved when she says nothing about them.

'I brought you in a couple of books and some of those awful boiled sweets you like. Are you in much pain?'

'I'm alright. They're giving me painkillers.'

She starts fussing with the water jug and some paper napkins on the side table. I know something is coming.

'I've been thinking that maybe you could come and stay with me for a while.'

'Thanks, but I have my own home.'

'I know, but those ribs are going to take a little while to heal. You're going to need a bit of care.'

'I'll be alright.'

'Letting people help you, Emily, isn't a sign of weakness. Everyone needs help sometimes.'

'I'm fine.'

'For God's sake, Emily, you're not. Look where you are. I know you wanted to work this out on your own, but I can't pretend any more that I don't know what's happening. I kept hoping I was wrong, but clearly I wasn't. That man you married is never going to change—and next time he could kill you.'

I feel the heat rise and know my face must be bright red. I'm so embarrassed.

'Can we talk about this when I feel better?'

'Emily ...'

'Please. I haven't got the energy today.'

She closes her eyes and lets out a huge sigh, but her nod is gentle.

'Tell me about the library, Colleen. What's happening?'

She looks down and brushes her skirt like she's smoothing out some creases. 'We don't need to talk about that today either.'

'I can cope. Tell me.'

'Well, the good news is that Mrs Finlay's grandson started up that crowdfunding page to try and purchase the library. I put in an application to the community trust board, and we have a raffle going and the tickets are flying out the door. The Knit and Natter group have already pledged fifty pounds. Amy Frecklington has donated five pounds from her pocket money and is urging the other kids at school to do the same. Even mean old Mrs Fagan put in a few pounds.'

'Mrs Fagan parted with some money?'

'Well, she pledged it, which isn't quite the same as handing it over. Mrs Johnson is doing a bake sale outside on Saturday morning, and Arlo is dropping some vegetables off for us to sell this afternoon.'

I look at her, and I know that she's holding something back.

'What's the bad news, Colleen?'

She lets out a sigh. 'There is already an offer on the table. We'll never raise enough money—and never by the deadline.'

'When is it?'

'Next Friday.'

'Will the annexe be ready by then?'

'No.'

Our gazes lock together, and there is nothing more to say. I shift in the bed, and a sharp pain from my ribs makes me gasp. The machine that holds my drip starts beeping. I'm grateful for the distraction of the nurse as she pushes a couple of buttons and checks the IV in my arm.

'Don't worry about the library, Emily,' Colleen says. 'You just have to concentrate on getting better.'

WILLIAM

I take the books individually from the shelves and thank them as I place them in a cardboard box. Each one conjures up a memory of a person, place or time. Sometimes, it would take me days to let go of the characters from the stories. They'd let me into their lives, and I felt bereft when they left.

I press a few to my chest and decide to make a pile of the ones I'm not quite ready to let go. I thought I could donate all my books to the library, but Colleen said we might not have one for much longer.

I hear my wind chimes in the garden, and I look out to see Arlo tapping on them and waving to me from under the apple tree. By the time I get into my coat and make it down to him, he's laid out a grand feast on a blanket. I settle myself down on some cushions under the branches; his gesture tears me up. The last of the setting sun is caught in the river as we sip our home-made ginger beer from champagne flutes.

'I went to the hospital and talked to Emily today.'

'Good. How's she doing?'

'Battered and sad, but I sensed that she's going to be alright. I told her about knowing her mum. About my part in her death.'

'Can you let it go now? I think you've punished yourself enough.'

'I know. I should have listened to you and moved on long ago.'

'Now you decide to listen to me.' He passes me a quince and mulberry tart. 'I harvested the quince a little early and made some jam. I'll get Marco to bring some over for you.'

'Thanks, Arlo. You've been a great friend.'

'And you.' We chink our glasses together. 'We never did make sense of the world.'

'No, I'm not sure if anyone can.'

As the sun sets, I take the metal box from under my bed. It takes all my strength to lift it up and take it out to the lounge. I take out the dozens of letters written to Emily, all started and never finished.

I kept telling myself I was waiting for the right words, but now I see I was stalling for time.

I struggled to write down the events that happened because some part of me still couldn't accept what was. Maybe if I had written them down, I wouldn't have been held hostage by the past for so long.

A gust of wind blows in as Marco bowls through the front door. The letters fly up in the air and then scatter on the floor.

'I've brought you some jam.' He looks at the letters strewn on the floor. 'Shit, sorry.' He starts picking them up. 'Where do you want me to put them?'

I point to the box but then change my mind.

'Would you mind burning them?'

'Sure. I'll put them in our incinerator tomorrow.'

'No. Would you mind burning them now, Marco? Throw them in there; I'm done with them.'

I point to the AGA and watch as Marco tips the box and the letters slide into the fire. They catch alight.

'I thought I'd have a go at cutting our hedge, William, but I can't find the loppers.'

'You're going to cut it?'

'Yeah. I promise not to cut it into a shape.'

I smile, remembering the time he chopped his father's hawthorn hedge at the front of their house into a shape that looked like an elongated penis.

'Thanks, Marco. I think I left them beside the garden shed, or maybe down by the apple tree.'

'You know I said that you did it, William.'

'Did what?'

'The penis shape.'

'Haha. Did you?'

'Yeah, I thought it was worth a shot. Dad didn't believe me, of course; he extended my grounding for another week for telling a lie.'

'You were such a funny boy. Some of the things you did had your dad and me in stitches. You were always thinking up schemes to get rich. Remember when you decided to breed and sell mice and then found out that the demand wasn't as big as you thought?'

'Oh, yes—don't remind me. I don't think Dad thought my schemes were very funny.'

'Oh, he did—but he had to put on a serious face. You're going to have to look after one another after I'm gone.'

'Don't say that.'

'Marco, we can all see what's going on. I don't have long.'

'I'm not really comfortable with this, William.'

'I'm sorry—but pretending just makes it harder for me. I need your help with some things.'

'Like what?'

'You know how I talked about selling the antiques?'

'Yes.'

'I've changed my mind. Other than one chest, I want you to have them all. But don't feel like you have to keep them, Marco. You can sell them and set yourself up in a business or something.'

'William, they'll be worth hundreds of thousands.'

'I hope so. Don't keep them sitting around gathering dust like I did. I kept them because they reminded me of my mum, but you don't need to do that. You don't need to see a piece of furniture to remind you of me.'

'William ...'

'Please let me finish. The library has a crowdfunding page. It's set up to raise funds for the manse so the community can keep the library. I offered them the Chippendale butler's chest in the back bedroom. I thought you could help by selling it for them.'

MARCO

I search William's face for any signs that he knows I'm involved with the sale of the manse. All I see are his smiling blue eyes and the familiar crinkle at the edge of his mouth, like he's about to laugh. He's laid his colourless hand on top of mine, and the contrast between the two makes me want to pull mine away. I want to carry on pretending that he's not dying, but he keeps making that harder to do.

'I'll see what I can do.'

'They need the funds by next Friday, so get whatever you can for it.'

'It's a bloody Chippendale, William. You don't just grab the first price you're offered. It'll need to go to an auction house.'

'I don't have time for that, and I don't think they do either.'

'Okay.'

'You could put it in your dad's shop over the weekend.'

'Yeah, I'm sure someone will give you a few hundred for an item that's worth thousands.'

'Every little bit helps. A village needs a library, Marco; like a body needs a heart.'

'Alright, William. I'll make a few phone calls and see what I can do.'

'Thank you, Marco. You're a good boy.'

'I'm not sure about that, but it seems I'm about to be a rich one, thanks to you!'

'Huh. That'll only get you so far. When you're dying, you know what really matters—and believe me, Marco, it isn't money.'

'Right. Is this where you give me my next life lesson, or a quote from one of your friends? I was starting to worry that you might be losing it. I haven't had a lecture for a few days.'

'They're not lessons. They're just thoughts.'

'What are your thoughts, then?'

'Connections are more valuable than money. Humans aren't meant to operate on their own. It's easy to shut down, but we need each other. I got lucky when I found you and your dad. You both helped me connect back in.'

'How?'

'You both thought the best of me. That's a great gift to give another human. Don't isolate yourself, Marco.'

'I'm fine, William. It's easier to be on my own. Anyway, I have you and Dad.'

'For the moment. What I'm trying to say is that things will never replace people.'

I hear in his voice that he's tiring. 'Alright, I think that's probably enough for the day. You rest now. I'll come back later, and you can torment me some more then.'

'Can you take that chest now?'

'Yes, if you promise to sleep.' He nods.

He's already asleep when I return with the chest from the back room. I pull a cover up around him, and have to swallow a huge lump in my throat as I leave.

I struggle getting the stupid chest through the hole in the hedge without scratching it. I have to leave it sitting out in the garden while I try to find the loppers. Finally, I see them resting at the side of the shed.

'What are you doing with those, Marco?' Dad calls out as he walks towards me.

'I'm just going to make the hole in the hedge bigger. Did you know that William wants me to have his antiques?'

'Yes. He talked to me about it. It's very generous—but, as he said, you're like a son to him.'

'That's the bit that makes me feel bad. He's always been there for me, and I've taken that for granted. I'm only just realising it now.'

'Least you've realised it. What are you doing with the chest?' He nods towards the furniture on the lawn.

'William wants me to sell it and give the money to the library.'

'That puts you in a difficult position then, doesn't it?'

I'm grateful for the fading light, and hope it hides the surprise on my face. I can feel Dad looking at me, but then he turns and walks away. The chest feels like it's doubled in weight as I drag it through the hedge.

EMILY

It's a funny thing when you realise that you've been listening to the wrong story your whole life. In one moment, everything you thought you knew turns out to be nothing but big fat lies. *Even your own mother ran off and left you* had been on repeat throughout my childhood, yet that was never the truth. Replacing the words *ran off and left you* with *was taken from you* changes the whole picture.

I imagine my fifteen-year-old mother cradling me and then someone ripping me away from her. That must have hurt her so much. But at least she got a chance to hold her baby; Rob stole that from me. I move my legs to the side of the bed, and a sharp pain just under my rib reminds me to move slowly. They're saying I have to stay for another week, but I don't mind if it's longer. There's always someone popping in to say hi, or to check on you. It's the first time in years that I've felt like I can think straight.

I take down the map of Scotland and fold it up gently. Even I know that 'I promise never to do it again' should only be used once.

I jump when I hear a noise. I'm surprised to see Colleen back.

'I just had to come and tell you,' she says with a huge smile on her face. 'We've just had the best news.'

'What?'

'The buyer withdrew his offer. Now we at least have more time to find the money.'

'Really?'

'Yeah. Apparently, the buyer's accountant rang Beatrice and gave her an earful. He said that he'd had a call from someone who told him that the building had suffered some major structural damage in the last storm. He said his informant was well acquainted with the building, and that he and his client didn't appreciate their time being wasted. They want nothing more to do with the sale.'

'But we didn't have any damage.'

'I know. It's strange—but it works in our favour. Nancy's the treasurer on the committee, and she came straight over and told me. She was one of the members who voted against selling the manse. She told me that the amount of money that our crowdfunding page has raised in such a short time surprised the other committee members. She said not only did it show them how much the manse means to this community, but it also made them think they could try crowdfunding for the church footings.'

'That's fantastic.'

'I know. All I need now is for you to get better so you can help us.'

'I will. I've been doing a lot of thinking while I've been lying here. I'd like to come and stay with you for a bit. If that's still okay.'

'God, of course it is. You can stay forever.'

'I don't need forever, but at least a few weeks. Enough time so Rob can move his stuff out.' I don't want the tears to come, but they do.

Colleen wraps her arms around me and lets me sob into her chest. For once she doesn't say anything, and just rubs my back until I finish crying. I feel the space between us grow smaller. She pulls away and kisses me on the forehead.

'You're doing the right thing.'

'I know, but it's hard.'

'Of course. You love him. But believe me, Emily, you can't change him. He needs some help.'

'He's not going to like my decision.'

'No, which is why you can't tell him alone. You need to let us support you. We can get the police to have a word with him.'

'I don't want the police involved. I don't want to press charges. I just want him gone.'

'Okay, but they'll let him know that charges will be pressed if he comes anywhere near you. Or I could kill him.'

'You don't need to do that. Don't worry, he'll leave me alone. He does know that what he's done is wrong.'

'I'm sure he does. It's just a pity that it doesn't stop him doing it.'

I'm grateful for the interruption when the tea lady comes in. I take the cup that Colleen offers me and sip the tea through the straw. 'I've been thinking about something else too.'

'What's that?'

'I'd like to sell my grandmother's house.'

WILLIAM

I think that if I write the end now, then, when it's time for me to leave, I'll be able to choose which story I want to sit in.

I wonder about that four-minute gap … after your heart stops beating and before your brain shuts down. Is this where we let go? Like the space at the end of an exhalation, before you take the next breath in.

When the pain gets too much, I ask Arlo to read to me. He chooses one of my books and flicks through the pages until he finds something he likes. He looks up at me once, then bows his head and starts to read. The words come through muffled. Like I've slipped into a warm bath and my head is submerged just below the surface. The past and the future fall away, and I hear a voice talking about the still point. That seems like a nice place to rest.

Acknowledgements

Many people have made this book possible. A very ugly first draft was produced at AUT as I studied for my Master of Creative Writing. Thank you to the tutors, but especially to James George who was my supervisor. Huia Publishers invest not just in a project but in their writers. I feel grateful to have them by my side. Thanks to the editing talents of Bryony and Daisy, the finished product reads so much better. Thanks also to the design team at HUIA and Catherine for her beautiful illustrations on the cover.